CYNTHIA HICKEY

KILLER POSE

A Hollywood Murder, Book 1

Cynthia Hickey

DEDICATION

To all the mystery lovers!

CHAPTER ONE

I clutched my camera, ready to start pressing the shutter button. Staying on my side of the red roped border, I stood in anticipation with the other paparazzi waiting for the arrival of megastar Brock Hanson and whoever was his latest arm candy of the moment.

A black limousine stopped at the curb and a man in a dark suit opened the car door. Before one finally dressed leg could emerge from the limo, the screams of fans filled the air. I rolled my eyes. Taking pictures of spoiled Hollywood royalty was not how I had envisioned my career going. I wanted to be a reporter. Still, if I had to work for a tabloid, Hollywood Tribune would be the one to work for.

Brock emerged from the limo and posed for the cameras, his killer smile in high voltage. He waved, then glanced around the crowd as if looking for someone. His gaze clashed with mine. He winked and smiled before turning to help a woman in a form-fitting black dress from the limo. They posed, waved, and strolled down the red carpet into the building amid screams and tossed roses.

Lauren Mayfield, Hollywood's newest star and, according to rumor, Brock's most recent love interest. Her smile looked pained. Of course, I didn't listen to gossip despite working for a tabloid. I sought the truth. Always. Someday, I'd work for a top newspaper and win a Pulitzer.

My boss had gotten me special privileges to enter the awards hall and interview the stars, Brock and Lauren. Surprisingly, they'd both agreed upon hearing it was me who would be doing the interviewing. I smiled. Perhaps my reputation preceded me. Most likely it was my father's career as a well-loved actor turned real-life detective that had them agreeing to see me.

I flashed my badge which proudly displayed my name, Kelly Canyon, reporter, to the guard at the door and entered through a back door. The fans outside might be in a frenzy at seeing their favorite stars walk the red carpet, but inside…the stars were just as excited. The air crackled with energy.

I located Brock's dressing room toward the end of the hall, rapped three times, and waited. Within seconds, Lauren, one hand clutching a glass of white wine, opened the door and ushered me in with a wave of her slender hand. I was petite at five-foot-two-inches and a hundred and sixteen pounds, but I felt like a moose compared to the almost anorexic frame of Lauren who stood at least three inches taller than me without her heels.

"Thank you for agreeing to meet with me." I perched on a straight-back chair and pulled a notepad from the over-sized bag slung across my shoulder.

"Not a problem." Brock smiled, doing funny things to my stomach. It wasn't hard to see why he'd been voted the world's most handsome man last year. Dark hair, bright blue eyes, and a million-watt smile.

Lauren sprawled across a deep green sofa. "Ask away. We have less than thirty minutes before we have to take our seats."

"My apologies." I glanced at Brock. "Have you always wanted to be a movie star?"

"Ever since I was three." He tilted his head and flashed that famous smile again. "I've always entertained…family, friends, strangers in the store. Acting is something I was born to do." He cut a glance at Lauren.

"What?" She frowned. "I'm not born to act?"

Uh-Oh. I detected tensions rising for reasons I wasn't aware of. "Miss Maxwell, what about you?"

She gave a sad smile. "I was discovered in a bar in San Diego. I wore lingerie as my costume. Because of that, I've been accused of sleeping my way to stardom." She tossed back a big swallow of wine.

"Did you?" My pen poised over the paper.

She shrugged. "I did whatever it took. Not everyone can be as lucky as dear Brock."

His face darkened.

I got the impression they didn't care much for each other and that their supposed relationship was nothing more than publicity. "This question is for both of you. Your movie, A Killer Pose, is a blockbuster. What do you think your chances of winning are?"

"We're up against a heart-wrenching drama," Brock said, "but I believe we have a good chance. Action films don't always score as well as tear-jerkers."

True. "Mr. Handsome, uh Hanson." For crying out loud, Kelly, you're a professional! "You're involved with charity work. What are you working on lately?"

"I'm helping Habitat for Humanity." He tilted his head. "Perhaps you should come help, too. We're building a house this weekend."

Lauren made a sound deep in her throat. "Why would any woman want to get her hands dirty hanging drywall?"

A muscle ticked in Brock's jaw. "It doesn't hurt to give back, Lauren."

"I worked hard for what I have."

"And steamrolled over other people to get

there."

"Don't believe all the stories of dumped wives and girlfriends, sweetie. I couldn't possibly have done all the things I'm accused of. I'm good, but not that good." She finished off her wine and poured another glass.

Brock stood. "Thank you, Kelly. I see you're allowed into the party later. We can continue the interview then. It's time for us to take our seats." Back in acting mode, Brock took the glass from Lauren's hand, offered her his arm, and together they stepped back into the hall and headed for the auditorium.

Thank goodness I had never aspired to be an actor like my father. Even he had gotten tired of the back-stabbing and made a name for himself in law enforcement, especially after Mom ran off. He'd immersed himself in his job. If he hadn't been killed during a bust, he might have run for office someday. I had too hard of a time pretending to like someone I didn't, as it was.

I took my place at the back of the auditorium and snapped pictures of other beautiful celebrities arriving, producers shaking hands, and seat-fillers with stars in their eyes. Those pictures were for me, not the tabloid. My favorite snapshots were of real people living their everyday lives.

The lights dimmed. The only bright spot in the room was the stage. The emcee came out, cracked a few jokes, and the awards ceremony began.

While Brock's movie didn't win best picture, he did walk away with best actor. Lauren, her smile strained, took home best supporting actress.

Afterwards, I stepped into the room where the party was being held, snapped more photos, and tried my best to be invisible. In my black suit, I was a spot on the sea of brightly colored, expensive gowns and tuxes.

"There you are." Brock approached and took my hand. "Come get something to eat. You've had a long day."

I pulled back. "I couldn't. This is for the nominees and winners."

"Nonsense. It's for everyone here." He handed me a glass plate. "Besides, half of these women will only have a bite. Most of the food will go waste."

The buffet consisted of everything from crab legs and butter to cucumber sandwiches. I spotted boneless chicken wings at one end. There was truly something for everyone. I put some shrimp and cocktail sauce on my plate, added some fruit, and searched for a place to eat.

"Standing room only, it seems." Brock pulled me to a relatively empty corner. "I requested you for the interview. Did your boss tell you?"

"Yes. Why did you?" I stared into his face.

"Because you're known for telling the truth and I admired your father for the same reason." He smiled. "I like that. So few people in this town are honest."

Lauren, now in bare feet, staggered in our direction. She poked Brock in the chest with one long scalloped nail. "I should have won best actress. You know that. What did you do to sway the vote?" Her words slurred.

"I have nothing to do with that, Lauren. Why don't you go to your dressing room and sleep off the wine?"

"Oh, you'd like that, wouldn't you? Get me out of the way so I can't tell everyone what a suck up you are." As if she'd just noticed me, she turned and grinned. "Brock deserted his pregnant girlfriend for his first acting role. Did you know that? Dear, sweet, Brock. Mr. Handsome isn't as squeaky clean as he would appear to be." She patted my cheek a bit too roughly and made her way, swaying, down the hall.

"Not true." Brock popped a popcorn shrimp into his mouth. "She's had too much to drink."

I studied his face. What if Lauren was right? If Hollywood found out that their golden boy was tarnished it would turn the town upside down.

"Stop looking at me like that." He set his plate down. "You're always searching for the truth. You'll find out soon enough that what she says is nothing more than a lie." He shook his head, shoved his hands into the pockets of his tux pants, and headed toward his dressing room.

What a strange evening. I'd done nothing but snap photos and eat, yet, I found myself with the beginnings of the biggest story of the year. I bit the inside of my cheek. Would Lauren reveal more information when she was sober or would she forget everything she'd said? It wouldn't hurt to ask. I'd be calling for an interview first thing in the morning.

I finished the few items I'd put on my plate, then set the plate on a sideboard. I weaved in and out of the mingling celebrities, snapping photos until 1:45 a.m. Fifteen minutes and the party would be over. I put my camera back into its bag and headed for the exit.

A harried looking man called out, "Does anyone have a key to Miss Maxwell's room? She isn't answering her door."

I turned, instincts kicking in that there might be a story in the making. "Brock Hanson, maybe?"

I followed the man down the hall. He knocked on Brock's door. Brock, dressed in designer faded jeans and a tight tee-shirt answered his door. His hair was mussed, as if he'd been sleeping. A scratch marred his left cheek.

"Yeah?"

"Do you have a key to Miss Maxwell's room?" The man asked.

"Sure." He pulled one from his pocket then

unlocked the dressing room belonging to the actress. He shoved the door open.

I gasped.

Lauren laid sprawled on a ruby red chaise lounge. Sticking from her neck were the remains of a crab leg.

CHAPTER TWO

"Close the place down," a security guard shouted. "Call the police.

I pulled my camera from my bag and snapped some photos before the guard frowned in my direction. I took one last closeup of the crab leg, snapped a quick one of the scratch on Brock's neck, then put the camera away. Obviously, some of my father's instincts had rubbed off on me.

I stepped into a corner and settled back to watch.

Brock plopped into a chair and buried his head in his hands. Occasionally, he'd look at Lauren, shake his head, and resume his distraught posture. Was his reaction real or acting? After all, he was a very accomplished actor. I hated to think he might have killed her, but the scratch on his cheek looked suspiciously like the rake of a fingernail.

When he glanced up again, he caught me

staring. He paled under his tan and looked away.

The police arrived a few minutes later and separated everyone into different rooms. Those milling about in the main party hall were told to make themselves comfortable. No one was allowed to leave.

I was put into an empty dressing room. Five minutes later, two officers in plain clothes entered, bringing chairs with them. They sat across from me and didn't say a word. Not being guilty, I didn't squirm, only smiled.

The woman said, "I'm Detective Lawrence, this is Detective Sawyer. What is your purpose for being here?"

"I'm the photographer."

"Paparazzi."

I waved a dismissive hand. "If that's what you prefer to call me."

Detective Sawyer narrowed his eyes. "Aren't you Detective Canyon's daughter?"

"I am."

Detective Lawrence glanced at her partner, then back at me. "Then you will have noticed things other party attenders didn't, I hope." It seems she couldn't help but add, "if you aren't the guilty party."

"There's no way Detective Canyon's daughter would kill anyone." Detective Sawyer shook his head. "Tell us what you saw."

"The party was just beginning to wrap up. I'd already put my camera away and was headed for the door when a man, about five-foot-eight, rumpled tan pants, green polo shirt, gray hair, rushed my way asking if I knew anyone who might have a key to Miss Mayfield's room. I mentioned Brock Hanson might. He did. When Brock unlocked the door, Miss Mayfield was as you saw her."

"Thank you for the description," Lawrence said, a bit too sarcastically for my taste. "We usually have to dig for it. Who is the man who asked about the key?"

"I have no idea. I focused mainly on celebrities while I was here."

She handed me a business card. "Call if you remember anything else. Oh, and make copies of all the photos you took. Deliver them to the precinct." She stood, glanced at her partner and marched from the room.

"You're free to go, Miss Canyon." Sawyer gave a thin-lipped smile. "I admired your father very much."

"Thank you." My heart lurched as it always did when someone mentioned my father.

I headed home, my mind whirling with the nights events. Brock was the only person I saw with a possible motive for murder. Lauren had promised to besmirch his name, thus ruining his good-boy persona. I still couldn't see him in the role of a killer.

Dad always said the motives usually had to do with love or money. Which one resulted in Lauren's death? Love? There weren't any signs of a man in her life other than Brock and I now knew that was only for publicity. They couldn't stand each other.

Money? Maybe. Lauren was bound to have a healthy bank account. Would someone want her dead for what was in it? That raised another why question.

Stop it, Kelly. You aren't a detective. Dad was. You're a tabloid photographer and nothing else. Still, I knew I'd follow the case of Lauren's murder very closely. I couldn't help it. Curiosity was a part of me.

I unlocked my front door and stepped into the hall. "Good morning, Grandma."

"I told you not to call me that. I'm much too old to be a grandma." Grandma Ruthie, or Ruthie, stepped from the kitchen wearing a sheer robe over a silk nightgown. A famous exotic dancer in the sixties, then starring in some movies, she still thought herself always on display.

"Why are you still up?" I hung my camera bag on a coat tree.

"I want to hear all about the party." She pouted her ruby-red lips. "I still don't understand why I couldn't have tagged along."

"I was working." Plus, Ruthie with her wild

clothes and died black hair would have been a distraction I didn't need. "Someone killed Lauren Mayfield tonight."

"What?" She put a hand to her chest.

"Yep. A crab leg in the neck."

"I've always said those things were dangerous." She billowed out her robe and took a seat on a dark red sofa. "That's why I always have the waiter crack mine. Who did it?"

"No idea." I sat across from her and removed my gym shoes.

"You should wear heels, dear."

"Not when I'm on my feet for hours." I sighed and leaned back. "I'm exhausted."

"Oh, no, you don't. I want to hear everything."

"There isn't anything more to tell. You watched the awards on television, right?"

"Yes, but it isn't the same. Tell me about the buffet." She reached for a slim cigarette from a gold case.

I laughed. Only my petite grandmother would care about food she wouldn't eat. I told her as many of the items as I could remember, then moved on to gowns, hairstyles, and jewelry. "I promise to let you look at the pictures as long as you wish once they're developed."

"I suppose that will have to do." She blew a plume of smoke into the air above her head. "Go to bed, darling. We'll talk more later."

Not needing to be told twice, I grabbed my shoes and dashed up the stairs. Sleep didn't come quickly. It snuck in and around details of Lauren's death.

I slept until ten a.m., waking to the sound of my cell phone blaring the tune to "We will Rock You". I fumbled for it, finally grabbing a hold and putting it to my ear. "Hello?"

"This is Detective Lawrence. Miss Canyon, we need those photos."

"I didn't get to bed until five a.m., Detective. Can't I bring them this afternoon?"

"Nope. There's a one-hour photo shop down the street. See you in ninety minutes." Click.

What an unfriendly woman. I flung aside the blankets and shuffled to the shower.

"Kelly, dear, I need a ride to the salon." Ruthie, hair in an elaborate updo, wearing a wild-print sheath dress from the sixties, sailed toward me as I reached the front door. "We'll take the Corvette."

As tempting as that was, I didn't have time. "I have to develop these pictures and get them to the precinct. I'm running out of time."

"Then, drop me off afterward. They'll squeeze me in." She pushed past me and headed for the garage.

I groaned, knowing the salon wasn't the only place she'd have me take her, and followed. Minutes later, we cruised down Pacific Coast highway with the wind in our hair. I'd begged Ruthie many times to let me have the candy-apple red, 1965 Corvette convertible, but she refused. She didn't drive or have a license, but she insisted on hanging onto the dream car.

We dropped the photos off at the one-hour, then I dropped Ruthie at the salon with the promise to pick her up before heading to the police station. I would be late and I had a feeling Detective Lawrence didn't have much patience for tardiness. But, she hadn't had to deal with Hurricane Ruthie, either.

When I did arrive at the station with a large envelope containing the photos, I was an hour late. The detective made me wait thirty minutes before exiting her office.

She stared at the pacing Ruthie who wore large sunglasses and a multi-colored scarf over her hair, then motioned me to follow. As did Ruthie. "Just Miss Canyon, please."

"I'm Miss Canyon."

"You're Mrs. Canyon, if my guess is correct."

"Same thing." Ruthie gave a bright smile and sat in one of the chairs across from the detective's desk. "I'm an asset, I guarantee it. I know all there is to know about everyone in Hollywood."

"Grandma, please." I sat in the other empty seat.

"Ruthie," she hissed.

I rolled my eyes. "Ignore her, detective." I slid

the envelope across the desk. "Anything else?"

"We'll be in contact after we look at these."

"Aren't you going to interview me?" Ruthie frowned.

"This isn't a newspaper. Call us if you hear anything." The detective stood, clearly dismissing us. "Oh, and Miss Canyon, don't leave town."

"Insufferable." Ruthie climbed into the car and slammed her door. "Lunch?"

"Sure." I headed toward our favorite restaurant in downtown Los Angeles.

The place was packed. The hostess led us to a booth near a window and handed us menus.

"We both want salads," Ruthie said. "And wine."

"Salad and water for me." I handed the woman the menu. As I did, I spotted Brock sitting alone in a booth across from us. He glanced up, seeing me at the same time.

He picked up his plate and slid into the booth next to me. "I need your help."

"Hello to you, too." I scowled.

"Well, hello, Mr. Hanson." Ruthie smiled. "I don't think we've ever had such a good-looking lunch companion."

"Ignore her." I scooted over a few inches. "What do you need, Brock?"

"Why are you always telling people to ignore me?" Ruthie crossed her arms.

"Grand…uh, Ruthie, because you're always talking nonsense." I loved her with all my heart, but most of the time I felt as if I were the parent of a promiscuous teenage girl.

Brock set an intense blue-eyed gaze on me. "I want you to help me find how who killed Lauren and clear my name."

CHAPTER THREE

"Why would I do that?" My eyes widened. "Why should I get involved? This doesn't concern me." I held up a hand when Ruthie went to interrupt.

"But, Kelly—"

"Ruthie," I warned. "I can't help you, Brock. I won't interfere in a police investigation. My father taught me that much."

Grandma tapped me on the head with the handle of her butter knife. "Listen up, buttercup. That detective told you not to leave town. That means you're a suspect, too."

"Ow. What?"

"You heard me." She waved the knife in my direction. "They only tell suspects, or persons of interest, not to leave town."

"What possible motive would I have?"

"Everyone knows you want a big story," she

said, wiggling her eyebrows. "Well, this is a doozie of a story."

"Yeah, what she said." Brock flashed a grin at Ruthie who blushed.

I couldn't believe I hadn't caught the statement. I must be tired. "That doesn't mean I need to help the number one suspect."

"Why not clear both our names at the same time?" Brock's brow furrowed.

"Because I'm not sure you're innocent. How did you get the scratch on your face?"

He sighed. "Lauren. We got into a fight before heading to our separate rooms."

I crossed my arms. "About what?"

"Her accusations about me leaving a pregnant girlfriend behind."

"You didn't?" Ruthie's eyes widened.

"Of course, I didn't! The girl doesn't exist."

He seemed to be telling the truth, but Dad taught me not to always trust a pretty face. I'd find out the truth one way or the other but for truth's sake, not Brock's. "I'll see what I can find out."

Ruthie clapped. "Yippee. I've always wanted to solve a murder. A real one and not just one on television."

"You were always the victim or the killer, Ruthie." I shook my head and straightened as the waitress brought us our salads.

"True, and that's why I'm qualified to help you

on this." She dug into her salad with gusto and motioned for a refill of wine. "I've read a lot of great crime scripts."

"Wonderful." Brock aimed that killer smile on me. "Where do we start?"

I cut him a sideways glance. He really was gorgeous. "Don't you have a movie to make?"

"Nope. The producer is holding off until I'm no longer a suspect." He shrugged. "Said he doesn't want to start all over half-way through if I'm found guilty."

"So, he thinks you did it?"

"No, he's just being safe. Movies cost a lot of money." He waved to the waitress. "Lunch is on me, ladies."

Cameras snapped and bulbs flashed the moment we stepped outside of the restaurant. Ruthie slipped her arm in Brock's and smiled and waved. She was in her element while I was not. I slipped back a few feet to use them as a shield. I preferred to be behind the camera, not in front of it.

To my right, a grim-faced Detective Lawrence and Sawyer watched. Lawrence gave a nod of her head, then turned and marched in the opposite direction. Ruthie was obviously right. I was a suspect or they wouldn't be shadowing me. Time to put to use what my father taught me.

"Come to our place," I told Brock as I took Ruthie by the arm and practically dragged her to the car. She continued waving until the paparazzi were out of sight.

Ruthie heaved a dramatic sigh. "That felt wonderful. It's been a long time since I've been in the spotlight."

"I've told you to go back into acting. There's no reason why a woman of fifty-eight who looks ten years younger can't find acting parts." I meant every word. Ruthie might be a bit ditzy and impulsive, but she was a beautiful woman.

She gave a secretive smile. "I called my agent last week. She set up an audition for tomorrow morning. That's why I needed a visit to the salon." She whipped off her scarf to show she'd gone back to her original blond color. "I'm no longer a dancer so I figured it was time to stop looking like one."

"I agree." I grinned and pulled into our driveway. Seconds later, Brock pulled in behind us.

His eyes widened in the doorway of our home. "Oh, wow, it looks like a …"

"Bordello?" I brushed past him and headed for the kitchen. "Ruthie likes the colors red and purple."

"She also likes fringe, I see. Lots of it."

"Oh, hush." Ruthie playfully slapped his shoulder. "A woman is entitled to surround herself with lovely things."

I questioned her taste but had learned a long time ago to let it go. If the décor got to be too much,

I retreated to my room done in soft blues and white. "Have a seat. I'll make coffee unless you'd prefer soda?"

"Coffee sounds great." Brock turned a chair backward and straddled it. "I haven't slept well."

"I can imagine." I plopped a pod into the Keurig and pulled a pad of paper and a pencil from a drawer. "We need a plan."

"To catch a killer," Ruthie said.

I cast an amused glance at Brock who stared at the tabletop as if very interested in the wood grain. "What's on your mind, Brock?"

"It's no secret Lauren and I didn't get along. At least not in the industry's eyes. Our fans thought we might fall in love." He sighed. "Is it wrong that I don't want to play the grieving lover?" He raised a tortured gaze. "I'm sorry she's dead, I really am, but…"

I wasn't sure the best course of action. "Would it hurt to look sad when someone brings up her death? You're an actor. Play a part." I handed him a cup of coffee, then inserted another pod for Ruthie before making one for myself.

In my cup, I added a liberal dose of cream. I preferred coffee with my cream and wasn't the bit apologetic.

I took my seat and picked up the pencil. "So, what do we know about Lauren?"

"Not a lot," Brock said. "She was a quiet

brooder."

"Explain."

"I'd catch her off somewhere in her head, a sad look on her face. When she would notice me looking at her, she'd put on a smile and adopt the persona she showed everyone."

"Sounds as if she had secrets. We need to find out what they were. Who disliked her?"

"Everyone." Brock shook his head. "She might have had a friend or two, but I'm not sure who they are."

"Find out." I made two columns on the paper, one for suspects, one for friends. I used the pencil so I could erase and transfer from one column to the other if I needed to.

"I need a reason to be in the studio. I can't use you, Brock, since production is on hold. Any ideas?"

He twisted his lips. "I'm doing a guest appearance on a sitcom. It's in a different studio than the one Lauren and I were filming in, but we could say outright that you're writing an article on Lauren's murder."

"Yes," Ruthie said. "Honesty is always best. Then, you could wander just about anywhere. Especially tomorrow during my audition. Everyone knows you follow me everywhere I go."

"That's actually the other way around," I said. "But, yes, we can try the honesty approach. It's no secret I want to be a reporter."

"You do?" Brock raised his eyebrows. "I didn't know that."

"We hadn't met until yesterday, Brock."

"I still knew who you were." He gave a lopsided grin.

I felt a flush of pleasure at his statement. "You did?"

"Sure. The Tribune always says nice things about me. When they said they were sending someone to photograph and interview us after the ceremony, I looked at the website and picked the prettiest girl there."

"I'm the only girl there." I ducked my head to hide my smile. Imagine, Brock Handsome, uh, Hanson, thinking I was pretty. Me, Kelly Canyon with the bit of an overbite and skinny frame. I weighed 116 soaking wet. Brock was always seen with voluptuous women on his arm.

Stop being silly. He was only flattering me because he wanted my help.

"Let's start writing down names. I can always erase. Who hated her the most?"

His brow wrinkled. "The producer seemed to think her a big pain in his rear. His wife, actress Maria Stock didn't care much for her. The cameraman was caught in a screaming match with her. I'm sure there are more, but those are the ones I know off the top of my head."

"Don't forget her husband," Ruthie said, tapping her temple with a manicured fingernail. "She didn't like people to know about Doug, but once upon a time she told me."

CHAPTER FOUR

Not only did I need to find out who Lauren's enemies were, I now needed to locate a husband. Ruthie did enjoy the debris left behind when she dropped a bomb.

I watched as Brock headed to one studio and Ruthie to a smaller building I assumed contained offices. With my camera around my neck and a large bag slung over my shoulder, I headed to a group of people in historical dress. A few feet away, I snapped a picture of the group, not wanting to leave anything to chance. What if the killer was among them?

When I spotted the detectives, I made a quick detour. The last thing I needed was for them to think I was doing the exact thing I was doing—investigating.

"Miss Canyon."

I cringed and turned to face Detective Lawrence. "Good morning."

The hard glint in her eyes clearly said she wasn't having a good morning. "What are you doing here?"

"My grandmother has an audition. I'm, uh, taking photos." Not a lie.

"Paparazzi isn't usually welcome on studio lots."

"I'm not here in any official capacity. Just passing time until my grandmother is finished." I forced a smile.

"You wouldn't be interfering in a police investigation, would you?"

"Am I a person of interest?"

She gave a curt nod.

"Then, I feel obligated to ask a few questions in order to clear my name."

Her eyes narrowed. "Then I must tell you that you are obligated to share any information you dig up. I must also tell you that if you obstruct my investigation in any way, I will arrest you. Do I make myself clear?"

"Most definitely."

Not looking as if she believed me, she left. A few seconds later, the two detectives moved past my little poor excuse for a hidey-hole, leaving me free to approach the acting group.

They eyed me warily. Not seeing any big-name faces didn't deter me. Sometimes those in the background knew the most.

I stood there like an idiot. I had no idea how to approach the subject of Lauren's death. Did I just blurt out my reason for being there? I opted for the idea we'd cooked up last night. "Hello, I'm Kelly Canyon and I work for the Hollywood Tribune. I'm writing an article on the death of Lauren Mayfield and I'm hoping some of you might know something...anything."

They stared at me as if I'd just sprouted tentacles from my head. One woman shook her head. "We don't talk to paparazzi."

"I'm not here in that capacity." I put on my most beguiling expression. "You all know what it's like to want to move to the next level in your career. That's all I'm asking."

"Fine." The same woman crossed her arms. "Make it fast. We're due on set in ten minutes."

"Great." I pulled a notepad and pen from the bag over my shoulder. "What did you think about her?"

"Couldn't stand her," a pretty young woman dressed as a saloon girl said. "She was a petty, conniving—"

I got the picture as most of the others said things to the same affect. Lauren Mayfield didn't let anything stand in the way of her success. The accusations ranged from sleeping her way to the top to breaking up marriages to sabotaging auditions in order to get a job she wanted. There weren't going to be just one or two suspects. I had ten right here. "Did anyone like her?"

Saloon girl shrugged. "Her makeup artist did. Her name is Amber Jacobson. I saw her go into Lauren's trailer earlier. Maybe she's still there." She pointed to a line of trailers.

"Thanks."

I strolled among the trailers, doing my best not to stare at A-list actors milling about. I also tried to look as if I belonged and walked with purpose until I spotted the trailer with Lauren's name. I took a deep breath and opened the door.

The first thing to greet me was the backside of a slightly plump woman. She straightened and whirled, putting a hand to her chest. "You scared me."

"I'm sorry. Are you Amber?"

"Yes, who's asking?" She turned back to the array of makeup on a table.

"Kelly Canyon." I glanced around the primarily white trailer. Very posh with leather sofas, a faux fur rug. The only spots of color were the articles of clothing tossed over every available surface. "I'd like to ask you a few questions about Lauren."

Her shoulders shook. "It's horrible." Once she'd regained her composure, she faced me. "What do you want to know?"

"I was told you're a friend of hers."

"I am. We were more than employer and

employee." She fell onto a sofa covered with clothes. "I hate the fact I'm now working to clean her trailer so someone else can use it." She motioned toward a chair. "Sit."

"Lauren doesn't seem to have had many friends, but do you know of anyone who would want to kill her?"

Amber covered her face with her hands and shook her head. "How can you say that? Everyone loved her."

"Other than you, I don't know of a single person."

She jerked and pierced a dark brown glare on me. "They're lying."

"Why would they?"

"Because they're all evil." She smiled. "Oh, all right, no one liked her."

"Except you."

"Except me." Her eyes welled with tears again. "I'm sure there are a few others, but I'm not sure who they are. They won't be the actors. If you want to find friends, you'll have to look at the normal people." She leaned forward. "Sometimes, Lauren gave them her castoff clothing. I'm sure there are some grateful people."

I didn't figure that many people would like someone just because they gave them the things they no longer wanted, but it might be another place to ask questions. "Where might I find these grateful people?"

"The cafeteria and janitorial staff." She leaned back in her seat. "Why all the questions anyway?"

"I'm doing a story on her death."

"How wonderful. She deserves to be remembered."

I cleared my throat. "Did you ever hear her mention a husband?"

She gasped. "Lauren was married?"

"It appears so. Any idea who he might be? All I have is the first name of Doug."

"There's a Doug Lincoln that comes around here sometimes. She always made me leave the trailer when a man showed up, so I don't know if he's her husband. He doesn't seem the type."

"Why not?"

"He was short and kind of homely. She tended to go for the good-looking men." She stood. "I don't want to be rude or anything, but it's going to take me a few days to clear all this out."

"Do you mind if I look around? Maybe I'll find a clue as to who her husband is."

Amber shrugged. "Knock yourself out."

I got to my feet and headed to the small bedroom at one end of the trailer. It was just as messy as the rest. I stood in the doorway and surveyed the small room. A set of dresser drawers were pushed against one wall, the drawers hanging open as if someone had hastily rifled through them.

"Was she always this messy?"

"Yep! Made my job difficult."

I shoved aside some clothes with my foot. A white ruffled photo album stuck from under the bed. I picked it up and perched on the edge of the unmade bed. I'd only turned a few pages when it occurred to me I held a gold mine in my hand. There were photos of Lauren with just about every leading man in Hollywood, plus one short little man. The same man who had asked me if I had a key to her room.

I bet I was looking at Doug Lincoln. I set the album on the bed and quickly took photos of each page. I would need more time than I had to really study them. I spent a little more time rummaging in the bedroom, then moved to the bathroom. I didn't see anything as helpful as the photo album.

On my way out, I paused in the doorway of the trailer. Instead of cleaning up, it sure seemed as if Amber were looking for something. Clothing flew over her head as she muttered words I couldn't understand.

There was more here than what it seemed, but Ruthie's audition would be over soon and she hated to be kept waiting. My gaze fell on a tabloid on the floor. On the front page was a picture of Brock and Ruthie under the headline "Does Brock Hanson have a new leading lady so soon after Miss Mayfield?"

"Disgusting, isn't it?" Amber snatched the paper from the floor. "The very day after Lauren's death he's moved on."

"No, he hasn't. That's my grandmother. We had lunch together, nothing more. May I have that?"

"Sure. I don't want to see it again."

With the tabloid folded and shoved in my bag, I hurried to the building where I'd left Ruthie. She held court in front of at least twenty-five people. Some I recognized from the big screen, others looked like workers.

I stood off to the side and let her revel in her moment of glory, praying she'd gotten the part she auditioned for. She truly was in her element here.

"Ruthie is something else."

I turned, coming nose-to-nose, literally, with Brock. My heart rate increased, and I took two steps back. "Yes, she is."

"Have you discovered anything interesting?" His eyes sparkled. Clearly, he knew how he unsettled me when he stood too close.

"Maybe. I do know who Lauren's husband was, or at least I strongly suspect. He was at the after-awards party."

An eyebrow arched. "He was?"

"Suspicious, isn't it?"

"Not if he works in the industry. What's his name?"

"Doug Lincoln, according to Lauren's makeup

artist."

"You met Amber. She's a bit odd, but nice enough." His brow creased. "The name Lincoln sounds familiar. I'll see what I can find out about him."

"Here." I pulled the tabloid from my bag. "You might want to see this."

"For crying out loud. This makes me look even more guilty." His shoulders slumped. "People are going to hate me. Do you know how hard it is to stay a nice guy in this industry? Then, some cold-blooded killer took it all away in a second."

"He also took a life, don't forget that." I frowned.

"See? Normally that would have been my first thought." He raked his hands through his abundant head of hair. I shook away the desire to run my own fingers through the dark strands. "Now, I'm only concerned about myself."

"What's this?" Ruthie snatched the tabloid. "Oh, how fun. Do you think people will really believe I'm with Brock?"

"No. How did the audition go?"

Her smile turned to a frown, then back to a smile. "I got the part. I'm the leading lady's mother, which is the second biggest female role. It's all about reconciliation before the mother dies of cancer. A real tear jerker."

"That's wonderful." I gave her a big hug.

"You're back where you belong."

"And I'm not going anywhere for a long time." She linked one arm with Brock's and the other with me. "Come meet my new manager."

"What happened to the old one? Didn't you say he called you?"

"Well, his assistant did. It turns out he died last year. Oh, there he is." She slipped free from my arm and waved.

The man I suspected to be Lauren's husband, and possibly killer, turned and returned the wave.

CHAPTER FIVE

"I think this story is best suited to someone with more experience."

I glared at Larry Richards, head editor of the Hollywood Tribune. "You can't. I have an inside scoop, having been at the party and discovered Lauren's body. I can do this justice." In more ways than one. Somehow, I'd find the true killer and expose him or her. "I shouldn't have said anything and just went ahead with the story."

"Wouldn't have done you any good. I've assigned it to Susan Gilroy."

"What?" I jumped to my feet. How could he assign it to my nemesis?

He shrugged. "She has the experience." He leaned his elbows on his desktop. "How about this? You both write the story. Whoever's is best gets the spot."

It would have to do. "It'll be my name on the front page." I grabbed my bag and camera and stormed to my desk, shooting a hostile glance in Susan's direction.

She smiled and gave me a finger wave. The witch. Although she was a beautiful witch with long silky black hair and almond shaped hazel eyes. Ugh. No matter. I'd get information without using flirtation. I had a brain.

My rear end had barely settled into my seat when she leaned over the cubicle. "Don't be upset, Kelly. Larry knows best."

I grinned and turned my chair to face her. "What you don't know yet is that we're both writing the story and the best one wins."

Her eyes narrowed. "Then it's war."

"I guess it is."

She looked away first and disappeared. Good. I didn't need to have her staring over my shoulder as I made plans.

I intended to head back over to the studio around lunchtime and buy a sandwich in the café. If I was lucky, I'd have the opportunity to ask the staff about Lauren. Then, I could wander around and see if there were any custodians in the area. It was a start. Until I had a substantial suspect list and started erasing names, I couldn't get too deep into the investigation.

The tapping of heels alerted me to the fact Susan was headed out. I grabbed my things and followed. I wasn't above a bit of shadowing if it served my purpose.

She didn't look back once as she headed to her little red mustang. She tossed a bag into the backseat and climbed into the driver's seat. I ran for my baby-blue Volkswagon. Catching sight of her pulling out of the garage, I increased my speed and gave chase.

No. She was headed for the studio. Did she have someone on the inside to give her access? I prayed she didn't.

I sped ahead, taking a short cut Ruthie had told me about, and whipped into the back parking lot. Grabbing my legs, I rushed for the cafeteria. Closed for another hour. Ugh. I turned, looking for someone to question.

Brock strolled toward me only to be intercepted by Susan who darted from between buildings like a feral cat. I didn't care. I marched toward them. Brock asked me to help him. I'd be darned if I'd let Miss Exotic Beauty squeeze her way in.

A middle-aged woman pushing a cart piled high with articles of clothing lost her grip and the whole thing toppled over in front of me. "Oh, no."

I glanced from her to Susan and Brock, then rushed to help. "Here." Together we got the cart righted and the items piled back on top. "There you go." I tossed her a grin.

"You're a real gem, sweetie." She shoved a strand of light-brown hair out of her face. "That

Miss Mayfield left these all over the place. Amber wants them collected right away so she can dispose of them according to the deceased wishes."

"Did you know Lauren personally?"

She waved a dismissive hand. "Heavens, no. That woman didn't give lower staff like me a second look."

I grinned. "Which means you saw and heard plenty."

"You bet I did." She laughed. "Oh, the stories I could tell."

"Would you? To me only? I'll buy you lunch."

"It's a deal. I'll meet you back here in one hour." She continued her path to Lauren's trailer.

Feeling better than I had at seeing Susan talking to Brock, I joined them. "Good morning, Brock."

He smiled down at me. "Hey, Kelly."

Susan's gaze flicked from him to me. "You know each other?"

Brock put his arm around my shoulders and gave me a squeeze. "We're friends."

The day grew warmer. Although his gesture wasn't flirtatious in the slightest, my skin tingled. I gave Susan a big grin. "The best of friends."

"Really?" Her eyes narrowed.

"Susan was just about to ask me some questions," Brock said, his arm returning to his side. "Go ahead."

"Where were you when Lauren was killed?"

"Asleep in my dressing room."

"Then?"

"With Kelly in Lauren's room."

Susan's gaze hardened. "Where did you go after that?"

"Home."

"And the next day?"

"With Kelly."

Susan reminded me of a cartoon character who had steam coming from its ears. "Just how much time do the two of you spend together?"

"Quite a bit," I said, my smile not fading. "My grandmother will be filming here in a week or two so we're always around."

"You aren't going to win this, Kelly." Susan squared her shoulders. "Just because your father was a well-loved detective in this city doesn't give you more credentials." She spun on a four-inch heel and tapped her way out of sight.

"What was that all about?" Brock's gaze followed her.

"We've both been assigned to write a story about Lauren's death. The best story gets published."

"We need to make sure yours is the best." He flashed a smile at me. "I've got to meet with the producer, but I'd like to buy you dinner. Meet me here at five o'clock?"

Be still my heart. "I'll be here."

I hung around the area not discovering anything new until my lunch date arrived. "I'm Kelly Canyon," I said.

"Mary Harper." She opened the cafeteria door and flashed her employee badge.

I hadn't thought of needing one. I wouldn't have been able to get in without Mary. I was doubly grateful I'd stopped to help her.

Once we'd moved through the line and filled our trays, me with a salad and fruit, her with fried liver and onions, gross, I paid for our meals. We chose a table in the back of the room. A few seconds later, I glanced up and spotted Ruthie's manager, Doug Lincoln.

"My grandmother just signed with that man. What do you know about him?" I squeezed ranch dressing over my salad.

Mary glanced over her shoulder. "Mr. Lincoln? He seems nice enough." She faced me and lowered her voice. "Was married to Miss Mayfield. Don't you think it strange he's at work?"

"Maybe they were estranged."

"That's putting it mildly." She laughed and cut into the liver on her plate. "He'd sometimes leave her trailer with his face as red as a stop sign. We never heard yelling, but it was quite plain they fought a lot and couldn't stand each other."

"Why stay married?"

She shrugged. "No idea."

"What about her and Brock Hanson? What type of relationship did they have?"

"Nothing off the screen. Miss Mayfield was a hard woman to like, may she rest in peace. While it's sad she's dead, it didn't come as much of a surprise to anyone."

I popped a strawberry in my mouth and once again settled my gaze on Doug Lincoln. Estranged or not, it did seem strange that he wasn't mourning, at least a little, the death of his superstar wife. I needed to find a way to speak with him.

"I know you work for the Tribune," Mary said. "Is that what this is all about?"

"Yes, ma'am." I faced her. "I'm trying to become a reporter. This is my best chance."

Her mouth quirked. "Some say you might have killed Miss Mayfield in order to get such a story."

My heart stopped. "Who said that?"

"Some dark-haired reporter is spreading that juicy tidbit around."

The only way Susan could have found out I was a suspect is if she'd spoken with one of the detectives. I intended to find out which one and raise havoc.

"I would never commit murder for the sake of a story." Although, I had to fight off the urge to strangle Susan. "Thank you for the information, Mary. I really appreciate it. Would you give me a call if you think of any reason or any person who would want to kill off Lauren?" I handed her a business card. "Please don't speak to the other reporter."

"I won't. This is between you and I."

"Thank you."

I hurried to my car and sped for the police department. My blood had reached the boiling point by the time I arrived.

I stormed in and demanded to see Detective Lawrence. The receptionist let her know I was there, then smiled up at me. "Go on back," she said.

"Thank you." I burst into the detective's office. "Which one of you told Susan Gilroy that I might have killed Lauren Mayfield in order to get a story?"

Lawrence's brows lowered. "Settle down, Miss Canyon. I haven't told anyone that bit of info. Sit down and stop accusing me of things before I find a reason to arrest you."

I plopped into a chair. "Someone told her because someone told me she did."

After staring at me long enough to make me squirm, she asked Detective Sawyer to join us. After he entered the room, she asked, "have you mentioned to anyone that Miss Canyon is a person of interest?"

"No, because I don't consider her one." He set his jaw.

"Hmmm. Well, someone is spreading it around.

Find out who."

He gave a nod, smiled down at me, then left us.

Lawrence crossed her arms and leaned back in her chair. "How did you find someone who knew that? Are you investigating?"

"Just trying to clear my name and write a story. Not because of a murder, but because I want to further my career."

"That could be a motive."

"It isn't." I met her stare.

"I hope not. Have you had a chance to look over the photos?"

"No." I'd been too busy running around the studio lot. "I'll do that tonight and let you know if I see anything suspicious. Although, I see no reason for you to believe a word I say since I'm a suspect."

Her gray eyes twinkled. "You aren't a suspect, Miss Canyon. Contrary to popular opinion, I do know an innocent person when I see one."

"Then why say I am?"

She leaned her folded arms on her desk. "Because if the killer thinks our attention is focused on you, they may make a mistake that lets us catch them."

I didn't appreciate being used as a scapegoat. "Fine. I'll help the charade in any way I can."

"Just try not to get yourself killed."

I stood. "Why kill the number one suspect? That would be a sure sign of my innocence."

She laughed. "You're a smart girl, Miss Canyon. Have a good evening."

"You, too." I headed back to the office to make sense of what Mary had told me and the detective's ploy to bring a killer into the opening.

CHAPTER SIX

I sat across from Brock at a hidey-hole burger joint feeling more at home in his company there than I had at the fancier restaurant. While we waited for Ruthie to join us, she refused to be left out when all of Hollywood thought her and Brock an item. Her words not mine. I filled Brock in on my conversation with Mary earlier in the day.

He slouched in his chair looking mighty fine in faded designer jeans and a light-blue button up shirt with the sleeves rolled up. "The only new news is that Doug is the phantom husband. I wonder how Mary knew and not everyone else."

"You'd be surprised at what the normal folks pick up. The snobby people don't notice them and speak as if they aren't there." I waved as Ruthie paused in the doorway.

After a few heads turned and one woman rushed forward for an autograph, Ruthie joined us. "It feels good to be back in the limelight."

"You can have it." Being one of the vulturous paparazzi, I knew I had no desire to be the focal point of anyone's attention.

"It isn't all that bad," Brock said, "if you keep your nose clean."

"Your's is a bit dirty right now," Ruthie said with a laugh. "Being the suspect in a murder has you on the front page of every tabloid." To prove her point, she pulled a few from her purse and tossed them on the table.

"Hollywood's Golden Boy loses his halo," I read. I cringed seeing Susan's byline under the photo.

Brock flipped through the stack. "This is horrible. How can my fans really believe I'd kill Lauren?"

"Oh, sweetie, everyone loves a bad boy. Look at this as good publicity." Ruthie motioned to the waitress. "You'll stay at the forefront of everyone's mind for months, even after you're proven innocent."

He didn't look convinced. "Kelly needs a way to question your manager."

"Why?" Ruthie cut me a glance.

"He's Lauren's husband, or he was." I perused the menu the waitress dropped on the table with a scowl at Brock.

"This sucks." His gaze followed her as she stomped away. "We need to solve this mystery fast."

"Poor boy." I smiled and decided on a mushroom and swiss burger. "Can you arrange a meeting, Ruthie?"

"Sure. He's coming over for supper tomorrow. I'd kind of thought I might want him to court me, but now I'm not so sure."

"He doesn't seem your type."

"Because he's average? That's exactly why he's my type. No need to be jealous." She never glanced at her menu, ordering a salad when the waitress reappeared. Once we'd given our orders and were left alone, she continued. "If definitely doesn't hurt a star to have their manager wrapped around their finger. I'm sure that's why Lauren married him. That and the fact the man is loaded, loaded, loaded."

Both mine and Brock's gazes snapped toward her. "How do you know that?" I asked.

She shrugged and grinned. "I asked my friend at the bank to look at his account."

"That's illegal."

She pointed a straw at me. "Only if you get caught. Sometimes you have to skirt the edges of the law in order to get information. Don't forget that while you're trying to find a killer."

Too much of my father ran in my veins to break the law, I hoped. While Detective Lawrence hadn't outright said so, I suspected she knew I was asking questions. I got the impression she encouraged me to do so. Would I stop if she ordered me to? I couldn't answer that.

Brock blinked a few times and shook his head. "I agree with Kelly. I can't add arrest to my list of non-existent crimes."

"Oh, pooh. You both are party poopers."

Our burgers arrived and for a while nobody spoke. I couldn't help but wonder what other connections Ruthie might have that could help us.

A young man from the Tribune stopped at our table and snapped our photograph. "Fraternizing with the suspect, Kelly?" He flashed a grin and raced away.

"Robby Thurston!" I took off after him. "You can not turn in that picture."

He stopped at his older model Toyota. "Why not? It's my job to take pictures of celebrities and there were two at that table."

"Because Larry won't like it."

"Not my problem." He wiggled his eyebrows and got into his car. "See you at the office tomorrow."

I scowled after him. Larry would think I was fraternizing with a suspect just as Robby said. Which I was, of course, but I didn't want it to affect my job. Which it would.

"What's wrong?" Brock stepped up behind me.

"I'm going to be in trouble at work. I should be

taking your picture, not having dinner with you."

"So? Take it now." He smiled and flipped my ponytail over my shoulder. "I'll call the Tabloid tomorrow and tell your boss that I hired you as my personal photographer until Lauren's murder is solved and that he cannot print anymore pictures of me without my consent."

"You'd do that for me?" Warmth filled me.

"Of course. That's what friends do for each other."

I doubted it would work, since the Tabloid wouldn't care if they had his permission or not, but the gesture was very sweet. "Thank you."

"Come and finish your burger. You can't do anything about it tonight." He put his hand on the small of my back and steered me to where Ruthie had a line of fans wanting napkins signed.

I sighed and slid into the booth. Brock chose to sit on my side rather than back with Ruthie. When the autograph seekers finished with Ruthie, they turned to Brock.

"Your signature will be worth even more than it is now if you're found guilty," a woman said. That only served to increase the line waiting at our table.

I groaned inwardly and focused on my food. How could anyone enjoy the constant attention? I was more than ready to leave by the time the line finished and ushered Ruthie to the car before anyone else cornered her.

"Don't be in such a hurry, dear. I can call Uber."

"Don't be silly. I'm right here." I tossed Brock a wave as we sped from the parking lot.

The next morning, Larry called me into his office as soon as I set my things at my desk. Sighing, and trying to ignore the satisfied smirk on Susan's face, I stepped into his office and closed the door behind me. "Yes, sir?"

He fixed me with a steely-eyed stare and slid the photograph of me eating with Ruthie and Brock. "Care to explain why you're with a murder suspect instead of photographing said suspect?"

"He's a friend of my grandmother's."

He cocked his head and raised his eyebrows. "I don't believe that for a minute. What are you cooking up, Kelly?"

My shoulders slumped. "He's asked me to help clear his name. Since I'm also a—"

"You're a suspect?" He stiffened. "Hanson called to ask that I assign you to follow him around, but this puts a new light on things."

I gave a slow nod. "Yes, but—"

He shook his head. "I'm putting you on administrative leave, Kelly, until you are no longer a suspect. This won't look good for our paper."

"What about the story?"

"You can still submit it when you're finished, and I'll pay you as a freelancer."

"I'm on leave without pay?"

"I'm afraid so. You signed a contract when we hired you that you would not shed the Tribune in a bad light."

"Fine." I whirled and marched from his office. I grabbed my things and stormed to my car. Without a job, I'd have to ask Brock to pay me as his photographer. I smiled as another thought occurred to me. I could always take photos of other stars as I was out and about and sell them to competing tabloids if Larry didn't want them.

With a bit of a plan to bring in some well-needed cash, I headed for the studio and the proposed meeting with Doug Lincoln. I parked in an empty spot in back. As often as I was there, the studio ought to give me an assigned spot.

I grabbed my bag and exited my car. Ruthie had said Doug's office was in trailer thirteen. Since I had a few minutes to spare, I headed for Lauren's trailer. The door was locked and a glance in the window showed everything had been removed. To where, I wondered? Had Amber found anything of interest? Most likely not. Why would the killer leave clues in the open?

I really needed to study the photo album and pictures of the party. I'd invite Brock over later and we'd go over them together. Between him and

Ruthie, they should be able to identify most, if not all, of the people in the photos.

Switching direction, I headed for thirteen and knocked on the door. Ruthie opened it and ushered me inside. My eyes widened at her bubble gum pink sheath dress and the bow in her teased black hair. "Is your part in the sixties?"

She narrowed her eyes. "No, I wanted to look girlie today." She lowered her voice to a growl. "Do not embarrass me."

No harm of that. "Thank you for agreeing to meet with me, Mr. Lincoln." I offered him a handshake.

He returned it with a limp-wristed one of his own. "You were there the night Lauren was murdered."

"Yes, sir. If you don't mind, I'd like to talk to you about that. I'm writing a story about her murder." I sat on a black leather sofa next to Ruthie.

"I don't see how this will help find out who took her from me." He sat in a rolling desk chair that matched the sofa.

"I'm here to clear my name, sir."

"Ah," he said, as if those few words explained it all. "I'll help in any way I can. Ruthie said you were trying to solve the murder. Why not leave it up to the police?"

"I lost my job."

Ruthie gasped. "No."

I nodded. "I can't work there as long as I'm a suspect." Which I wasn't, but I'd agreed to let it be known that I was. "Thus, my asking questions. I'll pass on anything of interest to the authorities."

"Very well. Ask away. I'm a suspect, too, as you most likely know."

"Some questions might be very personal."

He shrugged. "I've nothing to hide."

I didn't believe that for a nano-second. "Why did you and Lauren leave your marriage a secret?"

"We didn't. We simply didn't tell anyone. Some folks will think a manager plays favorites when sending clients on auditions if he has a personal relationship with them."

"How would you describe your marriage?"

"Up and down and twisting and turning like a roller-coaster." He stared over my shoulder at the window. "My dear wife couldn't be faithful if her life depended on it, yet I loved her regardless."

Her life most likely did depend on her faithfulness. "Any idea who she had affairs with?"

"Name any leading actor or producer and I'm sure they're on the list."

"Brock Hanson?"

"Some say so."

My heart fell, then lifted again as he added, "but I never believed that rumor. Hanson just isn't the type to go after a married woman. He's one of the last good guys left in this business."

He leaned on his desktop. "You might want to look at the producer and camera crew on her last film and on the one they had started filming. Lauren wasn't easy to work with and production always ran behind schedule. That might be enough motive for murder. Delays cost money." He rummaged in his desk drawer and pulled out a folder. "Their names are all here. Lauren always had me run background checks on everyone involved in her films. She said she wouldn't work with deadbeats."

"Thank you so much." I took the folder. "This is a wonderful lead."

CHAPTER SEVEN

With Ruthie clutching a glass of wine, Brock relaxing with a beer, and me sipping on a diet soda, we gathered around the kitchen table where I'd stacked the photos from the awards party. A bowl of popcorn sat nearby and fresh chocolate chip cookies from a bakery. If I hadn't made the popcorn, that would have been bought, too. Ruthie and a stove were not friends. Add microwave to the list. In fact, just about everything in a kitchen, except the wine fridge, could not be counted her friend.

"Let's take each photo one at a time and study it," I suggested, pulling one toward us. "If something seems off, one of us will see it."

The first photo was of Brock and Lauren exiting the limousine. Her smile seemed forced, but Brock's shined with good nature. I concentrated on the faces in the background. If some turned up more than others, they might be a lead.

"I couldn't recognize anyone in the crowd," Brock said, "but it's hard to see when flashbulbs are flashing in a person's face." He bent over the photo. "The faces are too dark."

"Well, I was focused on you and Lauren." I set the photo aside. The next one showed them from the back walking toward the building. More of the crowd was shown as people leaned over the red rope to get a better view.

Amber, Lauren's makeup artist watched intently from the sidelines. That didn't seem unusual to me. A man in a baseball cap pulled low over his eyes stood a bit behind her. It seemed cliché to think of him as a person of interest, but since he was also in the next picture, I tapped on him. "Who is this?"

Brock leaned closer. "I think that's Tony Lane, the cameraman on Lost in A Woman's Heart. That was the movie Lauren completed before starting on A Way Home. I think he's the cameraman on that movie, too."

I wrote his name on our pad of paper under suspects. While there were a lot of people in the photos outside the building, no one showed up multiple times except for Amber and Tony. The rest of the photos were of the party.

There were a lot of people in the photos taken before I interviewed Brock and Lauren. This time a regular face was Doug, again not surprising. I leaned closer to study the face of a man scowling in

Lauren's direction as she waved to someone off camera.

"Who is this?"

"The producer Louie Stock." From the sound of Brock's voice, he didn't seem to like the man.

"You don't like him?"

"He's a great producer, but he's the latest of Lauren's affairs. See the dark-haired beauty next to him? That's his wife, Maria, an up and coming star."

I added both their names to the suspect list. After all, the wrath of a wife toward a cheating husband had resulted in murder before. "Point out any other faces of friends or enemies. We'll worry about those we don't know later." I hoped we would find the killer among the people Brock did know. It would save a lot of time.

"I can tell you who some of those people are," Ruthie said. "For instance, that's Gary Porter. He was quite the leading man back in the day." She smiled. "He's my love interest in the film." She tapped another face. "That's Marilyn Carter. She's been known to play dirty to get a role."

Brock nodded. "I've heard her name from Lauren. She'd hiss like a cat when she said it."

Just like that I added two more names to the growing list in front of me. At this rate, we'd have everyone who'd ever said a word to Lauren on here.

Brock picked up a photo of him sitting across

from Lauren in her dressing room. His hair was tousled, his shirt unbuttoned. She lounged in a silk robe, one long leg exposed. It was a gorgeous picture, if I did say so myself.

"She seemed a little off that night. Now that the shock is wore off, I can remember a little better," Brock said. "When I asked her if she wanted to talk about it, she said no. I thought at the time it was because she didn't win best actress. What if she thought her life was in danger?" He lifted a tortured gaze to mine. "I could have helped her."

"You had no way of knowing." I put a hand on his arm. "Absolutely no way. If she wouldn't talk…"

"I wish she would have."

"Then you might both be dead." Ruthie refilled her wine glass. "Let's get to that photo album. I bet I can name everyone in there."

"You can start on that while Brock and I finish up here."

It didn't take long before Ruthie was crying and laughing simultaneously.

I shot Brock an amused glance, relieved to see the cloud of despondency lift from him. "I suddenly can't wait to look at the album."

"Me either." He snatched it from Ruthie's hand, laughing.

"Hey! I was reminiscing." She tried to take it back, only to trip over the edge of the rug, spill her wine down Brock's shirt, and land in his lap. It couldn't have been timed better if it had been written in a script.

Brock yelped and leaped up, dumping Ruthie onto the floor. He whipped his shirt over his head and dabbed at the spilled wine on the rug.

"Excuse me." Ruthie tapped him on the shoulder. "Help a lady up."

"Sorry." He stretched out a hand.

I had been nothing but a puddle of tears from laughing so hard at the comedy show in my living room, but that faded real fast when my eyes cleared and I got a look of Brock without his shirt. The man was the prettiest thing I'd ever seen.

"Put your eyes back in your head, girl, and get a towel." Ruthie scowled. "This is a Persian rug."

My eyes widened. My face heated. I turned and ran.

Brock laughed and headed down the hall.

When I returned from splashing cold water on my face in the kitchen sink and found a towel I didn't care if it got ruined, Brock was wearing a polyester shirt from the seventies. The man could look good in anything.

"Where did you get this shirt?" He frowned at Ruthie. "And how did anyone wear this fabric against their skin?"

"Oh, darling, I have several men's shirts hanging in my closet." She winked. "You never know when one will come in handy."

I cleared my throat. "Too much information. Let's look at this album without any shenanigans."

"Party pooper." Brock sent a slow, sexy smile my way.

Danger! I ripped my gaze away and stared at the wedding photo of a very young Lauren Mayfield. "They've been married a long time."

"Since Doug became a manager," Ruthie said.

"Why would anyone stay with such a cheater?"

"He was probably using her as his main cash source," Brock said. "At least in the beginning. She did quite a few B movies before getting a break."

I really hoped the man didn't marry my grandmother to have the same stream of steady cash. "How many clients does he have?"

Ruthie shrugged. "A lot."

Good. I wouldn't have to worry about her. Unless he was the killer. Then I'd worry a lot.

All of the former Hollywood greats were in at least one picture in the album. Some of them were still around like Gary Porter and Marilyn Carter. Others came and went, playing small bits in movies. There didn't seem to be anyone new to add to our suspect list.

We laughed until our sides hurt at some of the clothes. Ruthie would protest, saying they were the height of fashion of the time, but even she said she thought most of them atrocious.

"Now what?" Brock asked once he'd caught his breath.

"I head back to the studio and talk to the producer and the cameraman."

"That'll be easy." Ruthie drained her glass and set it on the table. "Those men are working on the film I'm in. Just come in with me. Since you lost your job, you have all the time in the world."

"You lost your job?" Brock straightened. "Because of me?"

"Not really." I closed the photo album and fingered one of the ruffles. "Since I'm a suspect, the editor thinks it reflects bad on the paper. I can still submit freelance photos and write the piece on Lauren, but I'm not on the payroll until the case is solved."

"You're too good for that place anyway." Ruthie patted my hand. "Try for one of the bigger papers."

I glanced up. "I'm thinking I might like to stay freelance."

"Wonderful. I guess I should start paying you rent."

I laughed. "That would be nice since you've filled my home with your…frills."

"This is my fault. I should not have asked you to help me clear my name." Brock sighed. "Didn't my calling and asking for you to be my exclusive photographer count for anything?"

"Maybe. I can still be your photographer. Since you're the number one suspect, all the papers will pay well for your photo." I wiggled my eyebrows and stood. "It's late, and every day seems a week long. I'll walk you out, Brock."

We stood on the front porch and stared at each other. I couldn't help feeling like a teenager on her first date. Silly, really. We were nothing more than two people tied together by a death. Until Brock lowered his head and kissed me.

I closed my eyes and leaned in, kissing him back until I came to my senses. Of course, if not for the car slowing down as it drove past, I wouldn't have any sense at all.

Pulling back, I peered through the night behind him. Oh, no. Detective Lawrence's face was lit by the streetlamp. This wouldn't look good. If she didn't count me as a suspect before, she might now that she'd seen me "fraternizing" with the number one suspect.

A light flashed, drawing my attention to the sidewalk where Susan and Robby stood. "Thanks for the picture," Susan called, before climbing into a dark SUV.

Could the night get any worse?

Yep. Detective Lawrence stopped her car and got out, marching toward us.

"I've some stupid suspects before," she said, opening the front door and jerking her head inside, "but the two of you are right up there at the top."

Shame faced, I stepped into my foyer, Brock on my heels. "Are you going to arrest us on suspicion of murder?"

She narrowed her eyes. "We've talked about that. I'm going to assume this is some part of your stupid plan. As for you…" she tapped a forefinger on Brock's head, "kissing someone so soon after your movie star girlfriend died is plain stupid. Your picture will be all over the papers tomorrow."

Brock wisely remained silent.

"That wasn't our fault." I crossed my arms. "Besides, Brock and I came up with a suspect list and motives. If you're nice, we'll share it with you."

Her eyes narrowed into slits. "You'll show it to me or I'll be anything but nice."

"Promise you won't take it?"

"Get. Me. The. List."

I rushed to the kitchen table, snapped a picture of the list with my phone, and hurried back, handing her the sheet of paper. "You are not a nice law enforcement officer."

"Never said I was." She turned for the door. "Try not to do anything stupid."

I looked up at Brock. "We need a picture to counteract the one Susan will send out. Do something sweet tomorrow when I have my camera."

He smiled, blew me a kiss, and sailed out the

front door.

My knees weakened, and I leaned against the wall, fanning my face.

CHAPTER EIGHT

After a reprimand the next morning from Detective Lawrence who informed me that, although I might not be a suspect I needed to act like one. Especially around Brock, the number one suspect. Nothing I said would dissuade her from her suspicions. Now, I stood in the doorway of Lauren's trailer, well, Ruthie's now and watched Amber spray something on my grandmother's face that smelled like roses.

"This is weird," I said, plopping onto the white sofa. "Doesn't it bother you to use Lauren's trailer?"

Ruthie frowned. "Why? She doesn't need it anymore."

Amber gave a nervous giggle. "It does seem strange, but I'm happy to have a job."

While Ruthie got made into the part she'd play, I glanced around the trailer. Other than the furnishings, there didn't seem to be a single item of

Lauren's left. "What did you do with all her things?

"I gave them to whoever wanted them," Amber said. "I kept a couple of things, but most were sold at auction. Something we're allowed to do if we want and since Lauren left me her personal belongings, I saw an opportunity to make a little extra cash. Most of them were purchased by employees, although a second-hand store downtown bought a few. Upscale Boutique, I think was the name." She shrugged. "Anyway, they seemed quite upset at not being able to purchase the whole shebang and said something about Lauren owing them."

Hmmm. I might have to pay a visit to the shop.

"You've bigger things to worry about." Ruthie pointed at a paper on the glass-top coffee table.

I picked up the Hollywood Tribune. Plastered across the front was a picture of Brock and me kissing. Across the top ran the title, "Top Suspects in Murder Case Make Lovey-Dovey". Seriously? Ugh. I tossed it at the garbage can. Susan needed better titles.

Sighing, I leaned back and watched Amber go to work spraying foundation on Ruthie's face to make her skin flawless. It took ten years off her life in five minutes. By the time Amber finished, Ruthie had been returned to her formal beauty.

"Ready?" She glanced my way and grabbed a silk scarf for her hair. "We start filming in fifteen minutes."

"I'm ready." I grabbed my camera and bag from where I'd set them on the floor and followed Ruthie.

She strolled to a waiting golf cart with all the ceremony of a queen. Some onlookers clapped, clearly happy to see her back in the acting world. Her smile outshone the sun.

I climbed onto the backseat and held on as the driver sped across the lot. As we passed Brock heading in the opposite direction, I tossed him a wave, which he returned with a big grin.

"Lovey-Dovey," he yelled after us.

My face heated. I had a horrible feeling that phrase would follow me around for quite a while.

The driver let us out in front of the studio and sped away. Doug waited at the door, holding it open for us. "Just in time," he said.

"Always," Ruthie replied.

Most often my grandmother arrived late in order to make an entrance, but I kept my lips clamped tight. No sense in putting her in a bad mood on her first day of filming.

I was left standing in the shadows as crew members and cameramen darted here and there in preparation to get started. Rather than approach anyone right off, I hung back and got a feel for those in the room.

It was clear to see who was the producer. A

large man, Louie Stock commanded those around him to follow his orders. A beautiful Hispanic woman sat in a director's chair and filed her nails. His wife, Maria, I assumed. There were several cameramen, so I had no idea which one was Tony Lane until someone called out his name.

A handsome man with dark blond hair turned and grinned. "Hey." He followed the other man out of sight. I now knew what three more of my suspects looked like. The problem now was how to approach them with questions about Lauren.

I remembered Dad once saying that a lot of detective work was observation. I perched on a crate, hung my camera around my neck, and prepared to snap whatever pictures I could without getting caught.

Once filming started no one paid me any attention. Louis barked directions. Since he was also producing the movie, he seemed a bit overzealous to me. One poor secondary actress ran off scene in tears.

"Get her back here!" Louis stormed in front of the camera. "You."

It took me a moment to realize he was talking to me. I put a hand to my chest.

"Yes." He shook his head. "I'm surrounded by imbeciles. Get up here."

"But I'm not an actor."

"You are now. Come play Ruthie's daughter.

That crying child is fired!"

I swallowed past the lump in my throat and let Ruthie's grin draw me like a beacon. I'd never acted before. I'd never had any desire to act. Someone thrust a script into my hand.

"Fifteen-minute break for the new girl to read over her lines," Louie said.

With those words, everyone skedaddled.

My legs gave way and I collapsed onto the sofa behind me. "I can't do this." I glanced up at Ruthie.

"Sure you can." She sat next to me. "It's very similar to our real life. I frustrate you, you want freedom, yada yada yada."

"I take pictures, Ruthie. I'm not in them." Ever since the awards party my life had spun out of control.

"If you don't do a good job, you'll be fired like the last girl. Louie is a tough man to work for."

"Great. I'll do a horrible job."

"And embarrass me?" She frowned. "I don't think so, young lady. Now, read and do your father proud."

Groaning, I read over my lines. Memorizing them wouldn't be a problem. I had a gift in that area. Ruthie was right. The role was eerily similar to our life at home. By the time the crew members returned, minus the girl whose role I'd been assigned, I felt as ready as I would ever be.

"Wait, wait." Louie threw his hands in the air.

"She needs makeup. Costume! What are you people standing around for? Get this girl ready."

To my horror, I was stripped and reclothed right there in the fake living room, then makeup hurriedly slapped on. No one seemed to think it a bit out of the ordinary.

"Why is her face red? Makeup!"

Amber rushed forward. "Stop blushing. You're ruining my job."

"I'm sorry. I've not stood in my underwear in front of twenty people before."

She shook her head as if I were an idiot and rushed away.

"Action!"

Blind me with a camera flash. What was I doing?

By the time the scene was filmed, I was more exhausted than I had ever been. Yet, a feeling of exhilaration rushed through me as people clapped me on the back for a job well done. Tears welled in Ruthie's eyes. I hadn't embarrassed her. In fact, it seemed as if I was a natural.

Doug Lincoln rushed forward with a contract, agreeing to be my manager without being asked, and had me sign to act in the movie. I was being paid a hundred thousand dollars and royalties. I had no idea if that was a going rate, but Doug said I couldn't worry about such things being a no-name. I signed, grabbed my camera, and got out of there.

Brock leaned against the outer wall of the building. "Welcome to my world."

"You heard?"

"Yep." He motioned his head to the side. "Everyone heard."

I followed his motion to see Detective Lawrence staring my way with a stony face. "Great." I approached her. "Make it quick. We're filming."

"You are determined to be in the spotlight, aren't you?"

"What better way to get behind the scenes where the murderer is most likely lurking?"

"Perhaps. Walk with me." She led me around the corner of the building. "I want you to look closely at Maria Stock."

"The director's wife."

"Her family does quite a bit of fishing in Mexico and supplied the crab legs for the party."

"She might have provided the crab legs in more ways than one."

Lawrence rolled her eyes. "Be careful and let me know what you find out."

"Is it normal to use a civilian this way?"

"No, but Detective Sawyer thinks you have your father's instincts and can be trusted to do a good job. I'm still undecided." She turned and marched away, leaving me to race back to the studio before our short break was over.

I got a glare from Louie for my trouble. We

filmed another scene and were told to go home until the morning. "Thank goodness."

"You did great, Kelly." Ruthie gave me a one-armed hug. "You have truly missed your calling."

I twisted my mouth. "Still not my cup of tea. I want to be a reporter."

"Just keep an open mind, dear. You might grow to love being in the movies." She grinned and sashayed out the door, calling over her shoulder, "find Brock. Dinner is my treat tonight."

"You are her real daughter?" I hadn't noticed Maria still sitting in the chair she'd claimed that morning.

"Granddaughter. I'm actually a photographer."

Maria's dark gaze settled on me as the lights in the room blazed to full life. "You do not look like her. But no matter." She got gracefully to her feet. "You did well. You should reconsider your career."

I was very close to getting tired of hearing those words come out of people's mouths. "No, thanks. I heard you supplied the crab legs for the awards party."

"Yes." Her eyes narrowed. "Why?"

"They were very delicious." I picked up my bag from the floor and slung it over my shoulder. "Very fresh."

"I will never eat one again. They are forever ruined by being used as a murder weapon on that horrible woman." She made a spitting motion on the floor.

I raised my eyebrows. "You didn't care for Lauren?"

"No. She was a tramp, and you ask too many questions." She stormed away on red stilettos.

That conversation didn't garner me anymore information than that one more person didn't like Lauren. I was starting to feel sorry for the woman. She must have lived a lonely life.

"Hey, you." Louie headed my way.

"The name is Kelly Canyon."

He blinked several times. "Are you Ruthie's daughter?"

"Granddaughter."

"Huh. I didn't think she was that old. Anyway, you did a good job, but I don't recall ever seeing you in acting before."

"You haven't. I came to watch Ruthie. My father acted a bit before going into law enforcement. Also, Ruthie is my step-grandmother which explains her younger age." Not that it was any of his business.

"Right." He grinned. "Rick Canyon. Well, I'll be glad to have his daughter on board." He clapped me on the back hard enough to cause me to stumble. "See you tomorrow."

He left, the lights went out, and I was left standing in the dark.

CHAPTER NINE

I'd fallen asleep the night before wondering what in the heck had happened with my life. I'd had plans. Plans I was moving toward completion. Now, I'd been kissed by a superstar, had a supporting role in a mid-budget film, and involved in a murder investigation. It was no wonder I woke up with grainy eyes and a headache.

"Up and at 'em." Ruthie banged on the bedroom door. "We need to be at the studio in less than an hour for makeup."

Ugh. I pulled the blankets over my head. I didn't want to act. I wanted to take pictures of those who did act, sometimes in hilarious or inappropriate ways.

When Ruthie's voice rose to a shriek and the pounding intensified, I threw back the covers and stumbled for the shower. A fifteen-minute stand under the spray had me a little more ready to face the day. Knowing the makeup people would change me into something they'd chosen, I pulled on a pair of faded jeans and a baggy tee-shirt. My hair went into its normal messy bun.

Ruthie frowned when I joined her in the living room. "Can't you at least try to put some effort into your appearance?"

"Why? They're just going to change it." I grabbed my bag and camera.

"But you should look good always. You're a movie star now."

"I highly doubt I'm a star. I'm a fill-in because the director was desperate. I just happen to have a knack." I hurried out the front door. "I thought you were in a hurry." I slid behind the wheel of the Corvette and turned the key in the ignition. I'd never get tired of the purr of the engine.

"At least we'll arrive in style," Ruthie said, sliding into the passenger side. She tied a scarf around her head. "Let's go."

We drove the coast. I wished we could take our time and just enjoy the ride. The car was made for cruising the Pacific Coast Highway.

We pulled into the lot and next to a waiting golf cart. The board man in the driver's seat straightened as we exited the Corvette. The moment we'd taken our seats in the cart, he sped across the lot and deposited us at Ruthie's trailer. Obviously, I didn't warrant a trailer of my own.

Amber greeted us with a scowl. "You're ten

minutes late. I need every minute I can get since they assigned me to both of you. Oh, and Kelly, you have a package on the table."

I had more than one actually. A large envelope contained my copy of the contract and a hefty check. I smiled and slid both into my bag. That would definitely help pay the bills until I got my job back. The other package was a white box tied up with a red bow.

I smiled, thinking Brock had given me a gift. I opened the lid and my smile faded. Inside, lay a black rose in the middle of what I hoped was splatters of red paint. Written on the inside of the lid were the words, "Stop asking questions." After the initial shock, I was actually pleased. Someone was running scared which meant I was getting close. I closed the box and placed it into my bag with my other things. I'd take it to Lawrence after the day's filming.

While I waited for my turn in the makeup chair, I read over my lines for the day. Ugh. I had a physical scene. Nobody told me I'd have to do any running. It seems my character liked to jog. I flipped through the pages. "This is a suspense?"

"Of course. You, my dear, have a stalker." Ruthie grinned. "Actually, we both do. It's your father who dumped us years ago and now wants our well-padded bank account. Isn't that fun?"

"Corny and cliché is more like it. Does my

character die?" I hoped. Then, my time in front of the camera would be less.

"Of course not. We're the main characters. I get to shoot the bad guy because he's holding you hostage."

Great. A B-movie. Well, Ruthie had to start somewhere in making her acting comeback.

Who could have sent me the box? I pulled my list of suspects from my bag. Who had access to the trailer? Amber, of course. I guessed the director would, and maybe his wife. The cleaning crew, definitely, but I didn't know any of their names other than Mary and she wasn't on my list.

"Where did you find the box?" I glanced at Amber.

"In your mailbox in the main building." She shook her head as if I were dense. "It's one of the jobs I did for Lauren. Check the mail."

The trailer door opened, and Brock poked his head inside. "Knock, knock."

"Come on in," Ruthie said.

"No, I'm in a hurry, but need to speak with Kelly for a minute."

"Hurry up," Amber said. "I'm almost ready for her."

I got to my feet. "We'll be fast." I stepped outside and pulled the door closed.

Brock took me by the arm and pulled me around back. "I was snooping around in the trailer where they keep props and heard a couple of workers talking."

"What were you doing in that trailer?"

"Looking for a bomber jacket I leant an actor for a movie. That isn't what's important here. One of the janitors said he'd heard that Maria, on a night where some of the actors hung around late for an impromptu party, threatened to make Lauren sorry. She'd had a few too many cocktails and they loosened her tongue."

"That is worth looking into. Who were the men?"

He pulled a piece of paper from the pocket of his jeans. "It took some digging into employee records but their names are Rod Looper and Ben Jones. I'm going to try and get them to talk."

"Good luck." I quickly told him about the box.

"I don't like that at all. Maybe you should step back for a while and let this person's attention fall on me."

I shook my head. "No, we're in this together."

"Kelly!" Amber's voice clearly said she was out of patience.

"I've got to go. I'll see you later this afternoon." I flashed him a grin and darted back into the trailer.

Amber slapped on an amazing amount of makeup considering I was going to be wearing a jogging suit and filming outside. We made it to the park with minutes to spare. Louie gave a strong huff from his nose, but didn't comment other than to tell me where he wanted me to start running.

Of course it was up hill and from the back, but considering my "father" would jump from the trees and give chase, it made sense. Action was called, and I took off.

A man I didn't recognize lunged at me from the trees. I stopped and reflexively swung my fist toward his head.

"Hey, that isn't in the script." He ducked.

"Cut!" Louie marched toward us. "What are you doing, Canyon?"

"I don't know this man."

"He's your father," he growled.

"How was I supposed to know that who was jumping out at me? I've not met anyone but Ruthie." I crossed my arms and glared. "Sorry, and nice to meet you…"

"David James."

"Can we start again?" I raised my eyebrows. "I promise not to try and punch you again."

He sighed and took his place while I resumed mine at the bottom of the hill. After five takes, I was out of breath, my headache was still in full swing, and I was hungry and cranky. Thankfully, Louie called a lunch break and I sat at a table set up for the actors. Someone brought me a sack lunch with a chicken salad sandwich.

David sat across from me. "I've never seen you

here before."

"I'm a reluctant participant. I actually came to write an article on the death of Lauren Mayfield and watch my grandmother act, when I got roped into this role." I bit into the sandwich which was amazingly good with just enough onion to make me glad I wasn't in a romantic role with anyone.

"Lauren was a good actress, but not well liked. I'm sure people will have plenty to say about her."

"I'm learning that. What about you? Could you be counted her friend?" I popped the tab on a diet soda.

"I'd like to think so. We starred in a couple of movies together. Since I'm not a married woman, I don't have a husband for her to steal if it helps her get ahead." He cocked his head. "You need to be careful. She didn't die by accident."

"I was there." I took a big gulp of the soda and held the cool can to my forehead. "I'd interviewed her."

"Now, you're here acting and she's dead."

"Thanks for the reminder." I stood and gathered my garbage. "Are you finished filming?"

"Until tomorrow. You are the lead in this movie, did you know?"

I froze. "I thought Ruthie was."

He gave a thin-lipped smile. "Louie must have seen something in you to put a no-name in a starring role even in a mid-budget film. See you tomorrow."

He gave me a salute and walked away.

I sagged against the table. The star? I groaned. It was going to be tough to say no the next time if I achieved any sort of fame, and I had a strong urge to demand more money for this film. Still, it was a job, for now.

When we finished for the day, I dropped Ruthie off at home and headed for the police station. The receptionist told me to have a seat and Detective Lawrence would be out when she finished with the person in her office.

Too bad I wasn't a novelist. The station had quite a few interesting characters walk through its doors. Prostitutes, druggies, a drunk…the people who made the world anything but boring. I pulled out my camera and snapped some pictures. They might not be movie stars, but they were more real.

"She's ready for you, Miss Canyon," the receptionist said.

When I stepped into Lawrence's office, her eyebrows rose to her hairline. "Stage makeup? From paparazzi to movie star."

"I didn't have time to wash my face." I pulled the box from my bag and set it on her desk. "I got this little present today. Sorry about my fingerprints, but I thought it was from a friend." I sat in the chair across from her.

The detective snapped on a pair of gloves before lifting the lid. "A definite warning." She speared me a glance. "Any other contact?"

"Nope. Just that."

"Who all did you talk to yesterday?"

I chewed the inside of my cheek while I thought. "Amber Jacobson, she's my makeup artist, the director, Louie Stock and his wife, Maria, a brief talk with cameraman Tony Lane, and Brock Hanson. That's it."

"Hmm. Are you sure Mr. Hanson isn't playing with your affections to take your attention off him?"

"I really don't think Brock is the killer, Detective." I sat back in my chair. "Are you familiar with the name Marilyn Carter? I heard that she and Lauren definitely did not get along and often fought over the same role. I haven't had a chance to talk to her yet, but I will."

Lawrence wrote her name on the desk pad on her desk. "Have you considered following in your father's footsteps?"

"Why does everyone want me in a job other than the one I want?"

She actually laughed. Not having heard the sound from her lips before, I joined in. "I just want to be a photographer for a newspaper. Paying the bills by joining the paparazzi squad is just for now."

"Have you considered the fact that maybe that isn't what you're meant to be?"

"Why do you ask so many questions?"

"Naturally nosy. It comes with the job." She

leaned her arms on the desktop. Her smile faded. "Be careful, Miss Canyon. Someone is watching you very closely."

CHAPTER TEN

After a restless night of wondering about my future, I decided to follow in my father's footsteps. He'd been a well-known star in Hollywood and chosen to do what his heart desired rather than listen to the crowd. I would do the same and continue toward my goal of becoming a reporter.

Being Sunday, Louie gave us the day off of filming. I grabbed my camera and bag and set off for Barry's Boot Camp. I needed some celebrity photos to sell if I wanted to keep my name alive in the business of tabloid gossip.

I leaned against a light pole across the street from the gym and waited. Waiting was a large part of the job, but patience always won. Today was no exception.

Marilyn Carter got out of a silver Mercedes. She wore tight yoga pants and a bright pink sports bar. Under the yoga pants was a very noticeable belly bump. If my suspicions were correct, the photo would be on the front page of every Hollywood tabloid.

She shot me a glare and hurried into the gym. I waited awhile longer, snapping pictures of a few lesser known actors before moving on. It was lunchtime and I'd agreed to meet Ruthie and Brock at The Ivy. I wasn't skulking around, but wouldn't pass down a profitable shot. Stars ate at the restaurant all the time. As for myself, I loved the country charm.

"Finally." Ruthie slid from her Corvette. "Of course, Brock isn't here yet, either. Doesn't he know you don't keep a lady waiting?"

"He'll meet us inside." I linked arms with her and entered the restaurant.

A hostess led us to a yellow room with blue and white plates covering the walls. I immediately spotted Doug Lincoln and a woman I didn't know at a corner table. I nodded in acknowledgement and took my seat. Using my menu as cover, I scanned the room.

Gary Porter sat at a table alone and hunkered over a lobster salad as if he hadn't eaten in days. I casually turned my cell phone in his direction and snapped a couple of shots. He'd almost finished before the woman who had sat at Doug's table moved to his. Gary frowned and straightened. It almost seemed as if he'd tried eating fast enough to escape before she joined him.

"Ruthie, who is that with Gary?"

She turned and glanced over her shoulder. "That's Iris Beacon. Old time Hollywood. We both tried out for the part of your mother and I won." She grinned. "She hasn't aged as well as I have."

"Why would she be meeting with Doug?"

"He's her manager, darling. Oh, there's Brock." She waved to get his attention. "God sure outdid himself on that man."

I agreed. Brock was definitely a work of art.

"You waited to order." He smiled and sat at the end of the table before motioning to the waitress. "I'm starved."

We chit-chatted about nothing in particular until the waitress took our order. During that time, the woman who had visited Gary stormed out of the restaurant with a very angry expression.

"Brock, do you know the story there?" I gasped as Susan's photographer snapped our photo after slipping money to the hostess. I knew first-hand how hard it was to get inside with a camera unless money exchanged hands.

"You've gone from pap to star," Brock said, laughing. "Welcome to our world."

"You can keep it." There was telling what lie Susan would come up with just to sell a paper. Before long, she'd write that Brock and I were engaged, or an item, something not true.

"As for Iris," Brock said, "word is she's scrambling. After her bout with alcohol and drugs, the industry is wary on casting her. She's done a few commercials but if you're in debt, as I've heard she is, that won't pay the bills."

"How did she feel about Lauren?"

"Sweetheart." Ruthie patted my hand. "Haven't you figured out yet that poor Lauren was not well liked?"

"Yes, but I haven't given up hope that someone made friends with her and that someone might suspect who hated her the most." I straightened while my California Cobb salad was placed in front of me.

The waitress fiddled with Brock's napkin, then his silverware, then set his glass of water just right.

"For crying out loud, girl, just ask for his autograph," Ruthie said. "He won't bite."

Brock signed his signature on the napkin, then handed it to the flustered young woman with a wink. "You might want to hold onto that for a while. It might be worth money someday."

She clutched it to her chest, nodded, and hurried away.

"She must be new." Ruthie frowned and watched the waitress until she was out of sight. "The staff here know not to treat us as other than normal people."

"There's a fundraiser on Friday night." Brock

cut into his salmon. "If you'd be my escort, Kelly, everyone who is anyone will be there."

"I'm going with Doug." Ruthie sat back with a grin. "Gotta make the man happy so he keeps getting me work."

I rolled my eyes. "I don't like fancy parties."

"It's not a party. It's a fancy dinner." Brock grinned. "It's for a children's charity. Five thousand dollars a plate. Come on. Be my date."

I sighed. If he was forking over that much cash to help kids how could I say no. "Fine." I pointed my fork at him. "But just as partners trying to find a killer, not as dates."

"Deal."

Great. Now I'd have to buy a gown.

After lunch, we parted ways and I went to Maxfield on Melrose Avenue. In the parking lot, I emailed the picture of Marilyn and her bump to my former boss, Larry and waited to see if he'd bite. He did offering me enough money to buy the dress I'd need.

Giddy as a schoolgirl, I entered the clean, fashionable store and headed right for Versace. I chose a black gown that fell to the floor in graceful folds. Spaghetti straps would keep it up and decent. Simple and stylish it would suit me for years.

Praying it would fit, I entered a dressing room.

"I told you no one can tell."

The voice of Marilyn drifted through the

partition. "I'm in very good shape. Who cares if that snip of an actress slash pap took my picture." Silence, then, "Look. I didn't get knocked up by myself. Unless you want me to tell your wife, you'd better lay off and pay off." She cursed, and I heard the door slam.

She was pregnant and by a married man. She wouldn't be able to hide the fact forever. I had more than one mystery to solve. One that would clear Brock's name and the other would get my job back. Maybe Larry would give me Susan's job and demote her to paparazzi.

I slipped the dress over my head and faced the mirror. I'd never felt more beautiful. The fabric skimmed my hips and accentuated my chest, giving me curves I didn't know I had. Delighted, not only with the gown but from what I'd overheard, I paid for the gown and headed home.

"I could have loaned you a gown," Ruthie said when I tried it on for her. "Why black? With your eyes an ice blue gown would have looked marvelous."

"Because I can wear this one multiple times. Black never goes out of style." I hung the dress in my closet. "I think Marilyn Carter is pregnant and I think the father is Louie Stock."

"That is news. How did you find this out?"

I told her about seeing Marilyn at the gym and the conversation in the dressing room. "The photo of her paid for this dress. I can't help feeling guilty."

"Don't be. Stars do that kind of thing all the time." She waved a hand in dismissal. "I wonder how they'll handle the filming of her movie. It's an action flick so it won't be easy to hide a baby bump in camouflage."

"I'm just thinking out loud so don't interrupt." I sat on the edge of my bed. "If Marilyn is pregnant by Louie, then she had to have been seeing him at the same time as Lauren, right? So that means Marilyn or Marie would both have a strong motive to kill Lauren. But..." I held up a finger, "here's what doesn't make sense. Why? People in this industry sleep around all the time."

"That's not true." Ruthie's brows drew together. "The tabloids spread that garbage around and it does sell papers, but most people here are good people. You just got thrust into the bad."

"Good. I was really starting to doubt mankind had any redeeming qualities left."

"But you are right about those two women have motive. What next?"

I fell back onto the bed. "I have no idea."

"Why not just ask Marilyn outright? You did hear her conversation. Anyone could have." She held her hand out in front of her and studied her nails. "I need a manicure. Those girls know everything that goes on around her. I bet they might have info."

"It's worth a try."

Thirty minutes later we sat in massage chairs while our feet soaked in salt water and girls wearing masks did our nails. They spoke Vietnamese. Which meant nothing. I threw out my lure.

"Did you hear the gossip about Marilyn Carter?"

Ruthie's eyebrows rose. "What? Oh, no, do tell."

"She's pregnant by the man who was seeing Lauren," I whispered.

"Louie Stock," the nail tech said in the same low voice. "Not new news."

"Really?" I acted shocked.

"Those women come here all the time. They fight."

"Mayfield and Carter?"

She shook her head. "Mayfield and Mrs. Stock. One not know about the third."

The girl doing Ruthie's nails spit something in Vietnamese and my girl got up and moved to another customer. I guess gossip was forbidden in that particular salon. An older woman with an impassive expression took my hand rather roughly in hers and started applying polish.

No matter. I'd learned that Lauren and Marie had allegedly not known about Marilyn. That meant Marilyn and Marie were my number one suspects. I couldn't wait to give the information to Detective Lawrence.

Which didn't take long since she was waiting at the house for us. She glanced at the cotton between our toes which were barely covered by thin plastic flip-flops. "Must be nice. Miss Canyon, do you have a moment?"

"Yes, and I was going to come by the station later. Have a seat on the porch." I waddled to one of the lawn chairs. "What's up?"

"You were seen again with Mr. Hanson."

"We're friends, Detective."

"I've also told you it isn't wise to fraternize with a suspect."

"Let me stop you right there." I filled her in on all I'd learned that day. "So, that makes Marilyn and Marie the most likely. Brock has no motive." I started to cross my arms, then remembering my nails, laid them on the armrests of the chair.

"They may have a motive, but it was Hanson who had seen her last."

"That we know of. He was sleeping in his dressing room."

"So he says."

I leaned forward. "Look. We can do this back and forth thing all day, but unless you're going to arrest me for spending time with Brock, then lay off. I'm attending a charity function with him Friday."

She smiled. "Good. I was going to get you an invitation. Now I don't have to. Keep your eyes and ears open. You got another threat today. A neighbor called it in." She directed my attention to the end of the porch where a skull and crossbones had been spray painted in red.

Great. A pirate wanted to kill me.

CHAPTER ELEVEN

I chose not to say anything to Ruthie about the painted warning. Instead, I applied a fresh coat of paint to match the rest of the porch and went to bed.

When I woke, I found my grandmother staring out the window at the porch. "Why the fresh paint job?" she asked. "We had it done two months ago."

"I couldn't sleep." I poured myself a cup of coffee.

"You're a terrible liar, but go ahead and keep your secrets." She shrugged and sat at the table, picking up the latest edition of The Hollywood Tribune. "Look. You made the front cover again."

I peered over her shoulder. Yep, there we sat with me gazing at Brock like some love-sick calf. The photographer had known exactly when to snap the photo. The title read, "Suspects in Stars Murder Get Cozy," byline Susan Gilroy. I wanted to strangle her. "Garbage."

"You work for this garbage."

"Not anymore." I was starting to wonder if I wanted to go back. Maybe I'd go work for the competitor, The Hollywood Enquirer. In fact, the more I thought about it, the more the idea appealed to me. If Susan wanted competition, I'd be happy to give it to her. Just as soon as my story on Lauren's murder was chosen over hers.

"It's going to be a beautiful day," Ruthie said, tossing the paper on the table. "Let's cruise the coast. We've been working hard and could use a day of fun. Maybe we can stop at Huntington Beach and get our feet wet. I'll call Brock and invite him."

Within the hour, Ruthie had situated herself in the backseat of my car, leaving me and Brock in the front. I didn't care as long as I got to drive. With the sun shining, a slight breeze, and a relatively open road in front of us, we headed up the coast.

Since the ocean was on our left, we couldn't see a whole lot, but I'd turn us around past Monterey and then we'd have some great views. Grinning, I placed my left arm on the doorframe and one hand on the wheel and let the wind pull my hair from its holder.

"You love this, don't you?" Brock grinned at me.

I tried to ignore how delicious he looked with his own hair blowing and a tank top showing off his chiseled arms. If I didn't, I might run us off the road. "I could drive this car all day. When Ruthie dies, she'd better will it to me." I laughed.

My backseat passenger slapped me on the top of my head. "I don't plan on dying anytime soon, girlie."

Exchanging a grin with Brock I turned around at Monterey and headed back down to Huntington. I took a deep breath of ocean air. Life didn't get much better.

"Not to ruin the day," Brock said, "but have you learned anything new?"

"Only that Marilyn Carter is pregnant, possibly by Louie Stock."

Brock looked shocked. "She's jeopardizing her career. Do you think she killed Lauren? It would cut down on the competition and being pregnant, Marilyn might do anything to get access to the baby daddy."

"It does sound like a strong possibility. Or," I held up a finger, "Marie killed Lauren to get her out of the picture. I heard Marie didn't know about Marilyn."

"She will soon if she doesn't."

"No work talk, you two." Ruthie leaned on the seat between us. "I'm thinking you should watch the road. I'm pretty sure we're being followed."

I glanced in the rearview mirror. "Why do you say that? We're in a no passing zone. Of course, they're following us."

"All the way from Monterey?"

"Sure." Although the heavily tinted windows of the SUV sent shivers down my spine.

Several cars passed us going the opposite direction. The SUV hit our bumper dispelling my idea that all was innocent. I pressed the gas pedal.

The other vehicle did the same pulling alongside of us and inching us toward the cliff on our right. "Ruthie, get your seatbelt on."

"Nope. If we go over that cliff, I want to be thrown free not die in a fiery explosion. Besides, seatbelts are confining."

"Hold the car steady," Brock said. He put a hand on my leg. "You can do this, Kelly. Remember who your father is."

The SUV rammed the side of my Volkswagon. Ruthie got to her knees on the backseat. "This car is priceless, you fool!" She shook her fist, ducking to the floor as the car swerved. Then she got back up yelling threats.

"I'm going back there to restrain her." Brock climbed over the seat leaving me alone.

He was right. Dad told me what to do in such a situation. Sometimes, when we sat on the porch, we talked what-ifs.

I pressed the gas again, shooting us forward. The SUV did the same. I slammed on the brakes, letting them shoot ahead, then pulled in behind the other vehicle. Staying in the center of the road, I prevented them from playing the same trick I did.

"Well done." Ruthie clapped.

Despite the grin on my face, my heart threatened to burst loose and fly into the ocean.

Once we drew closer to civilization again, the SUV turned and sped away. My heart rate returned to normal by the time we reached the beach. Anger replaced the determined fear as I marched around the car. Deep scrapes marred the paint.

"It's nothing that can't be fixed," Brock said, putting an arm around my shoulders. "Things could have been a lot worse."

"Yeah, we could be dead," Ruthie said. "Look how wrinkled I am from Brock forcing me to wear a seatbelt." She frowned down at her silk blouse.

"I need to find out who wants me dead."

"What?" Brock turned me to face him. "You've gotten more threats? Did they say they would kill you?"

"Not in those exact words, but trying to run us off the road seems pretty clear to me." I put my hands on my hips. "I'm getting close to finding out who killed Lauren. The only good thing about that SUV trying to wreck us is that the police can't look at you as a suspect anymore." I'd gone from trying to clear mine and Brock's name to finding out who the killer was before I became the next victim.

Later that day, Lawrence listened to my account of the day. Her face hardened, but she kept silent until I finished. "Yes, this pretty much clears Hanson. The fact you got the license plate is tremendous help."

"Considering I stared at it for several miles makes it less of a feat."

"Most people wouldn't remember after a scare like that."

"Good thing I'm not most people." I pushed to my feet. "I won't stop asking questions, Detective."

"I know. I've heard a lot about your father since I've worked here. You are his daughter, after all." She smiled. "Be careful and don't interfere with our investigation."

"I'll do my best."

By the time, Ruthie, Brock, and I dropped the vehicle off at a mechanic, called Uber and arrived home, I got a phone call from Lawrence saying the SUV had been stolen from Seal Beach earlier that day and abandoned a few miles from its original spot. That lead had led nowhere.

I plopped on the sofa and sulked while Ruthie ordered Chinese takeout. My gaze fell on the photographs and albums I'd moved to the coffee table. The secret to all this lay there somewhere. I knew it.

"What are you thinking?" Brock leaned in the doorway, one ankle crossed over the other.

"That we're missing something right in front of us." I sat back and propped my feet on the table. "We have three women after the same man. That means, in theory, that one of the two remaining women, or the man, is the killer."

"How are you going to prove it?"

"Keep asking questions until they confront me, I guess."

"Which scares the bejesus out of me," Ruthie said, joining me on the sofa. "I think you should back off and let the authorities handle this."

"You were all for it at the beginning."

"That was before we almost died in a fiery car crash."

I exhaled heavily. "You're right, but I can't stop now. It's gotten personal."

The doorbell rang. "I've got it." Brock answered the door, paid the delivery, and set the bag on the table before sitting in a chair across from us.

"It's time for you to use your charm, Brock." Ruthie opened the bags and pulled out the white boxes, handing each of us our order. "Few women can resist a face and body like yours. Woo Marilyn and Marie. See if you can't get them to open up. Kelly needs to cozy up to Louie."

"What?" I cocked my head. "I have no idea how to go about that."

"True. You have failed miserable at flirting in the past."

Brock cleared his throat. "I don't feel right leading these women on. Won't I be pretending to be the same type of man they're already fighting over?"

"You'll be acting, Brock." Ruthie shook her head. "As much as I hate to say this, Louie won't look at a woman my age no matter how attractive that woman might be. Kelly will have to do this. You've proven you can act, so act."

"I almost wish we'd gone over the cliff." I grabbed a pair of chopsticks. "Fine. I'll try." I shuddered.

"If Kelly is willing, then I'll see what I can do." Brock looked as if he shared my sentiment.

Not that he and I were a romantic couple, but knowing he wasn't a playboy warmed my heart. I was growing to enjoy his friendship and was glad to see he had scruples. "So, how do I go about getting Louie to talk?"

CHAPTER TWELVE

It didn't matter what I wore for my "flirtation" day with Louie. Amber would just change me into whatever I was supposed to wear for the day's filming. Not that I knew what to wear in order to get a man to talk.

"Smile," Ruthie said as we stood outside the studio door. "Make eye contact as much as possible. When you aren't flashing him a grin, act shy or coy." She fingered my shoulder-length hair. "I wish it were longer, but toss your head and flip your hair anyway."

"Like a horse?"

She groaned. "I guess that is how you would describe the action." Her gaze flicked to my chest. "I wish you'd been better blessed in certain areas. Men like a well-endowed woman."

I rolled my eyes. "Let's get this over with." I shoved open the door and marched inside. I was half-way across the room before I realized my mission. I tossed my biggest grin in Louie's direction.

His eyes widened, and he froze half-way to sitting in his chair. He gave me an uncertain smile in return.

Several times during filming, I smiled in the director's direction, causing him to call cut more times than ever before. "Stop looking at the camera, Canyon!"

"Sorry," I simpered. I was so bad at this. "Maybe I need private coaching?" I winked.

"Hanson!"

Brock stepped from the shadows. "Yes?"

"Take this woman to another room and give her some lessons in how to act on the set. Be back in thirty minutes." Louie stormed from the set.

Brock started laughing the moment we were alone. "You weren't kidding. You really are bad at the act of seduction."

"Spare me." I plopped onto a dark green sofa. "This is a stupid idea anyway."

"Regardless, we've said we would do it. Now," he sat next to me, "don't look at the camera. Do your flirting in-between takes. Watch how I do it with Marie."

I narrowed my eyes. "Why are you here anyway?"

"Nothing better to do. I need to start filming or lose my mind from boredom."

"You could wander around the lot and question the workers. Focus on catching Lauren's killer. You might be in the clear, but there is still someone harassing me."

"True." He pushed to his feet. "Filming will more than likely resume soon. I'll wander around after lunch. Right now, you need to be taught the art of flirtation." He held out his hand to pull me to my feet.

"Great." I'd rather have a tooth pulled.

Back on the set, I smiled at Louie, peering up at him from under lowered lashes. He still looked as confused as a turkey in a show bird event.

Brock leaned against the wall a few feet from where Marie glared at me. She, at least, knew I was trying to flirt. When Brock brushed against her shoulder as he bent to pick up a pencil from the floor, her attention got instantly diverted.

She returned the lazy smile he gave her, not looking away even when he did. Brock continued to send her short glances and sexy smiles until the woman started fussing with her hair and rearranging her dress to show more of her legs.

Good grief. I definitely didn't have the same appeal that Brock did. He was a sleek panther on the prowl while I was nothing more than a hyena failing at the hunt.

By the time lunch was called, my stomach growled loud enough to be heard and I made a beeline for the spread on a table against the far wall. I hadn't filled my plate before Louie sidled up next to me.

"I get the feeling you're trying to tell me something," he said in a low voice. "Care to tell me somewhere more private?"

"Oh. Uh." Come on, Kelly, you can do better than a few mumbled words. I forced a smile. "I was beginning to think you weren't catching my clues."

"I couldn't let the others be suspicious of my interest."

"Especially your wife."

He glanced over to where she laughed at something Brock said. "She's occupied at the moment. Follow me."

Feeling very much like I was about to enter a den of a master lion, I motioned to Brock to let him know where I was headed and followed Louie. He held the door open to a small office, complete with a desk, chair, and a large black leather sofa.

"Make yourself comfortable." Louie sat on the sofa and patted the cushion next to him.

Swallowing past a suddenly dry throat, I nodded and sat as far from him as the sofa would allow and concentrated on my chicken salad sandwich.

Louie took the plate from my hands and sat it on the desk. "Time for eating later. Let's get to know each other a little more."

"No, I'm hungry." I reached for the plate only to

find myself pushed back on the sofa until I was practically lying down. "I'd rather take things slow, Louie." I put my palms flat on his chest and shoved. "I don't fool around with any director of a movie I'm in."

His eyes hardened. "You haven't been in any movies."

"It's a new policy." I rolled off the couch and picked up my plate. Perching on the corner of his desk, I fixed a stern gaze on him. "What if we aren't compatible? Then, you will have angered Marie for nothing."

He wiggled a finger at me. "You're up to something, but I'll play along. What do you want?"

"I heard a rumor that you're the father of Marilyn Carter's unborn baby." My smile at his shocked face was genuine.

"Nobody knows that. You're blackmailing me?"

"No, no." I shook my head. "I'm writing an article on Lauren's death and you seem to be entwined with every angle of my story." I wiped my fingers with a napkin. "See, I know you had an affair with Lauren and Marilyn while you're married to Marie. It's quite the triangle. Did you kill Lauren to keep her quiet?"

"Of course not." He bolted to his feet.

I slid to the other side of the desk. "Who do you think did?"

"I don't know, nor do I care. Lauren was a

menace." He crossed his arms. "I'm not going to hurt you, Kelly."

"Tell your face that." I picked up a paperweight with a scorpion preserved in the middle.

He sighed and opened the door. "I'd give up on the art of seduction if I were you. You're horrible at it."

I skirted around the room and scurried out the door. "Are you sure you don't have any idea who killed Lauren?"

"Check out the other two women in my little circle." He slammed the door in my face.

That didn't go well. I wasted no time in letting Ruthie know her silly idea had fallen in a pile of dust at my feet.

"Hmmm." She crossed her legs and popped a strawberry in her mouth. "Maybe Brock is having better luck."

"Nope." He fell onto the sofa we'd use for filming later. "She says she doesn't know a thing other than her husband is a cheating blankety blank, but she wouldn't commit murder to keep him." He lowered his voice. "She also said she filed for divorce yesterday, but he hasn't been served yet."

"That doesn't sound like a killer. Someone willing to commit murder wouldn't file, would they?"

"It could have been a crime of passion," Ruthie pointed out. "Murders are always about sex or money. In this case it might be about both. I've spent a little time with Doug and it seems Lauren had him sign a prenup when they got married. He still has plenty of money, but she was spending hers faster than she could earn it." She studied her nails. "She also went away last year for a few months to have a baby that wasn't Doug's. My guess? She tried to blackmail the father and he killed her."

I met Brock's gaze, then turned back to Ruthie. "Who is the father?"

She shrugged. "Doug isn't sure. Said it could be Louie's or Tony's. Anyway, the child was left with Lauren's sister in Kansas."

"That's a lot of speculation," Brock said.

"It's all we got." I glanced up as Louie entered the room and approached Marie. In his hand was a large envelope. It seemed he'd been served. "I think we're finished filming for the day."

Yep. Louie told us all to go home.

I lingered a moment to see whether the situation would grow volatile. It didn't. Louie did nothing more than pace the floor and shout.

Brock and Ruthie waited for me outside. "What now?" Ruthie asked.

"I have no idea." I climbed onto the backseat of a waiting golf cart. "It appears we've reached a dead end. I don't know of anyone else to question."

The driver turned in his seat. "About the article you're writing?"

"Yes. How did you know?"

"Everyone knows that you and that snooty Susan are in competition. No one will talk to her, but I'll drive you to your trailer and tell you what I know."

True to his word, Frank, as he identified himself, entered our trailer with us and grabbed a soda from the refrigerator without asking. He popped the tab, guzzled half before coming up for air, and flipped a kitchen chair around and straddled it.

"If you're only going to tell us about Lauren having a baby or that Marilyn is pregnant, save your breath," Ruthie said. "We already know. What we don't know is who killed Lauren and who is threatening Kelly."

"Ruthie, that isn't common knowledge." I glared.

"Mum's the word," Frank said. "One of the girls who cleans the trailers overheard Marie threatening to kill Lauren if she didn't stop seeing Louie. This was right before Lauren went away last year."

"Did anyone else hear her say this?" I asked.

"That makeup artist of hers. That girl was Lauren's shadow." He folded his arms on the back of the chair. "I'm not saying Marie killed Lauren. People say things all the time. But, she did threaten to and when Lauren returned the director's wife was in a rage." His smile faded when he looked at me. "I wouldn't ask anymore questions of the director, his wife, or Miss Carter. One of them is a killer, I guarantee it. If you're getting threats, well…"

"I get your point. Thank you for the information." He hadn't told us anything new other than Marie threatened Lauren. That didn't make the woman a murderer. "Please let us know if you hear anything else."

He stood. "I'd talk to the makeup artist if I were you. They know just about everything that goes on around here." With those words, he left.

Brock frowned. "Do you think Amber might know something she didn't tell us? She gave us the photo albums. If she knew something, she would have told us then."

"You'd think so." I leaned back against the sofa cushions and pulled my cell phone from my purse on the floor. They weren't allowed on set. I had a text message from the detective telling me the paint from the porch was standard spray paint you could buy just about anywhere. Another dead end.

I rested my head back. We were absolutely nowhere on solving Lauren's murder.

"Chin up, Buttercup." Ruthie patted my cheek. "Sooner or later, you will come face-to-face with the person threatening you. When you do, you will have found the killer."

"Wow, that's a relief."

Ruthie laughed, but Brock's face darkened. "I

don't want you alone, ever."

"Don't be silly," Ruthie said. "If she isn't alone, the killer will never come forth."

"That's what I'm afraid of," he said. "The killer facing her alone."

He wasn't the only one.

CHAPTER THIRTEEN

The night of the fundraiser arrived. To say I was anything but excited would be a lie. But, I had to admit to myself, I looked fabulous.

I twirled in front of my mirror, smiling at the flip of fabric around my ankles. I'd slid my feet into a pair of ruby-colored heels and let my hair fall to my shoulders. The gown skimmed my hips and hugged my torso. I felt like royalty and couldn't wait to see Brock's reaction. At that moment, I was a star.

"Oh, darling." Ruthie clapped. "You are old Hollywood glamorous."

"I feel it." I grabbed a clutch that matched my shoes and headed downstairs to wait for Brock.

A limousine stopped in front of the house. Brock, sexy as all get out in a black tux, got out and approached the front door with a bouquet of roses. "For you ladies," he said with a grin.

"Thank you for picking us up in style," Ruthie

said. "I'll put these in water and we can go."

When she'd headed to the kitchen, Brock's gaze ran slowly over me, heating me from the inside out. "You are the most gorgeous thing I've ever seen."

"Stop it. You're lying, and I appreciate it." He'd had better looking leading ladies, but I could hold my own that night.

The ride to the banquet hall was filled with Ruthie's chatter as she speculated on what others would wear. She wore an iridescent gold gown with a small train, looking more Hollywood glam than I could.

"I am the luckiest man," Brock said. "I'll have a beautiful woman on each arm."

My face flushed. "Remember the real reason we're here. To find out who killed Lauren."

"Party pooper." He exited the limo and held his hand out to help me.

Flashbulbs lit up the night like fireworks.

"Brock, how do you feel now that you're cleared of murder?" one paparazzi called out.

"Are you and Kelly Canyon an item?"

"You didn't wait long after Lauren died to move on."

Questions and remarks peppered the air around us. With his hand on the small of my back and Ruthie's arm linked through his free one, we hurried down the red carpet and into the hall.

Getting a first-hand taste of the persistence of

paparazzi, I was more than happy that I'd never stooped to more than snapping photos. Brock was an expert at tuning out the personal questions.

We paused to catch our breath, then swept into the hall to look for our table. The place was packed with A and B-list actors. Ruthie strolled ahead of Brock and I, her smile firmly in place.

Our table was in the center of the room off to the right. Strangely enough, we were seated next to Louie and Marie. The tension was thick enough to cut off my breathing. But, I was an actor now and as such acted happy to see them.

Louie ignored me. Marie glared at me, smiled at Brock, and air-kissed Ruthie's cheeks.

Once the formalities were taken care of, Marie turned to me. "Why are you asking questions of my husband about Lauren's murder? He isn't a killer. Just a cheater."

"I heard you filed for divorce."

"So?" She pulled a compact from her purse and touched up the scarlet lipstick on her lips. "I can still look out for him."

"I don't need your help." Louie motioned to a passing waiter and snagged a glass of champagne from the man's tray. "Bring me scotch on the rocks. I'm going to need something stronger than this."

"Forgive me, Marie, but I've been assigned the job of writing about Lauren's murder. Since she and Louie were…" I cleared my throat. "I thought he might know of something, anything, that would help me."

"I'll tell you the same thing I told Brock. We don't know anything."

I picked at my napkin. "I'm in possession of Lauren's photo albums and it seems as if all of you were close once."

"We were until she went after my husband. Brock, sweetie." She put a hand on his arm. "Please call off your bull dog. Tonight is supposed to be fun."

"Louie!" Susan rushed toward us. "I am so sorry to hear of your impending divorce." She cut a glance at Marie who rolled her eyes. "I'm here if you ever need to talk."

It was clear now that papers were filed, Marie could care less who went after her husband. Susan patted his cheek, sent me a sly smile, and hurried away on the pretense of working.

Good luck. I had a first-hand seat at asking questions. As an actor, I could pretty much go anywhere on the movie lot I wanted to. As press, Susan was limited. I grinned and lifted my water glass in a toast to the back of her head.

"I do not like that woman." Marie tossed her dark hair over her shoulder. "I hope you win the silly competition."

"Does everyone know we're competing?"

She nodded. "I wish I knew something to help

you."

I sighed. "Me too."

Marilyn Carter and a man I didn't know sat in two of the empty chairs. Since Ruthie didn't have a plus one, the seat next to her would remain empty. A fact she clearly wasn't happy with. Her gaze flicked from one of us to another and she frowned. "This will not work at all. I must find a man. There. Doug." She left, only to return minutes later with her manager in tow. "He'll be joining us. Now, the night will be more enjoyable."

A dinner of steak and lobster was served as an older man stood behind a podium and gave a very long speech about the necessity of funds for the children's home and to thank us all for our contribution.

"That's William Johnson," Brock said softly. "He owns half of Los Angeles, or so the rumors go. He also owns the movie lot."

"Is he honest?" I fixed my gaze on the man.

"I've not heard anything to the contrary."

"He's as dirty as they come," Louie said, seeming to realize he wasn't at the table alone. "He'll chase any woman he sees then tosses them aside. I highly suspect Lauren had approached him for a loan recently. That man does not loan out money."

My suspect list grew by one. I watched as Johnson stepped from behind the podium and strolled through the crowd with a beautiful blond, young enough to be his daughter. As if he felt my stare, he turned, caught my gaze, and smiled before continuing to his table at the back of the room.

"Why isn't he sitting up front?" Ruthie turned in her chair.

"He usually leaves early," Louie said.

"Excuse me." Finished with my very delicious, and expensive dinner, I took my clutch to the ladies room, checking out each room down the hall as I went. If Lauren had approached Johnson and he refused her, would she have had information on him to blackmail him? I realized the thought came out of nowhere, but Lauren's lack of funds seemed to keep popping up.

I pushed on a stall door, only to find it shoved back at me. I hit the wall behind me and slid down the tiled wall to the floor. I caught a glimpse of white canvas shoes with a splatter of red paint before the door hit me again, slamming my head into the wall. The sound of running feet, then the slam of a door, let me know I was alone.

I got shakily to my feet and put a hand to my forehead. My fingers came away bloody. Wonderful.

Glancing in the mirror, I was shocked to see a purple bump already rising. I wet a paper towel with cold water and held it to the bump with one hand while the other hand shakily repaired the damage to my hair.

The lights went out.

Literally, when someone hit me in the back of the head.

When I came to, Ruthie and Brock both stood over me with identical worried expressions on their faces. "Hello," I said.

"You're lying on the floor of the ladies room and all you can say is hello?" Brock helped me to my feet.

"Why are you in here?" My head swam.

"Ruthie came and got me when she found you." He closed the lid on one of the toilets and sat me down. "We've called the paramedics."

"I don't need them. I need to punch the person who hit me."

"Oh." Ruthie put a hand to her throat. "I thought you'd slipped and fallen. I've already filed a report with Mr. Johnson."

I frowned. "That was fast."

"Not really. He came in as I rushed to get Brock. He said he'd take care of everything."

"I intend to." Johnson stepped up behind Brock. "How are you doing?"

"My head aches in the front and the back." I promptly vomited all over Brock's shoes.

"Everyone step back." Detective Lawrence and Detective Sawyer crowded around me. "We can't get medical attention in here with this many people in the way," Lawrence said as her partner shooed everyone away.

Brock refused to leave, but did step back to clean off his shoes.

Lawrence kneeled in front of me. "Quickly tell me what happened before the paramedics get here. I don't want the entire place to know."

"Someone hit me with the stall door, then when I was taking care of the bump, the lights went out and someone hit me in the back of the head."

"Got it." She moved back as two paramedics tried to squeeze into the stall.

The woman shook her head. "Can you step out here, please?"

"Gladly." I accepted her offer of help and staggered from the stall. The paramedic dressed the wound on my head, checked the bump on the back, and advised I go to the hospital as I most likely had a concussion.

"No, thank you. Brock will take me home. I can rest there."

"Do not let her go to sleep for an hour." The paramedic muttered something about stubborn actors, then followed her partner from the restroom.

On the way home, I laid my head against the back of the seat and closed my eyes. Brock moved my head to his shoulder. "Don't go to sleep, Kelly."

"I won't. Who was the first person on the scene?"

"Mr. Johnson," Ruthie said. "He was right outside the bathroom."

Unless he'd changed his shoes and snuck past us to hide in the restroom, he wasn't my attacker. "Then he might have seen who hit me. Do either of you have his phone number?"

They both said no, leaving me back at square one. "I'm sorry about your shoes, Brock. They look expensive."

"They are, but don't worry. They hurt my feet anyway." He chuckled. "You sure know how to liven up a dull party."

"Yep, that's me, the party girl." I closed my eyes again only to have Ruthie shake me awake.

"I won't have you dying on me, Kelly."

"I'm not going to die, although I'd sure feel better if I did."

"Not funny." She crossed her arms. "I don't want you doing this anymore. You came face-to-face with the killer and almost got killed. You still don't know who the person is."

"I know it's a woman, or at least a man with smaller feet. They wear white canvas shoes with red paint on them. That's more than I knew before getting my head bashed in."

"That doesn't seem worth it to me."

"Sure it is," Brock said. "If we find the shoes, we find the killer."

CHAPTER FOURTEEN

Since Louie decided it would be too difficult to disguise the bump on my forehead, he decided to film scenes without me, giving me time off. So, I sat outside a favorite shopping mall and waited for a celebrity to stroll by. It occurred to me that I spent a lot of time waiting on opportunities.

Ruthie, her arm linked with Doug's came my way and I snapped their picture. Ruthie grinned, Doug glared.

"Do not send that photo anywhere," he said once they got close enough.

"Why not? Ruthie is an actress making her big comeback. The papers will love it."

"Because my wife just died."

"Darling." Ruthie gave his arm a squeeze. "Your estranged wife. Besides, gossip sells papers and makes celebrities famous. You go ahead and sell that picture, Kelly."

Doug didn't look appeased in the slightest. "It's

bad for my reputation. People will think I'm an awful person."

I couldn't help but think his being a suspect was far worse than being seen getting cozy with my grandmother. Catching sight of the cameraman, Tony looking suspicious as he walked across the street, head down, hat pulled low, I decided to follow him and let my grandmother calm down her boyfriend. If that's what Doug was. I couldn't be sure. Ruthie liked men, plain and simple and flirted and cozied up to them all. None of them should take her seriously unless she wore their ring on her left hand.

Tony ducked into men's clothing store. Deciding to wait outside, I sat next to a fountain where I was partially hidden by a plastic fern. I didn't wait long.

He exited the store, no bag in hand, and quick-stepped back the way he'd come. Normally, I wouldn't consider that weird behavior since I lived in Crazywood, but being smack dab in the middle of trying to keep someone from killing me—I questioned everything. Especially when that someone wore white canvas shoes.

I'd said I didn't think it would be a man hiding in the women's restroom, but it could have been. Tony wore white canvas shoes. I needed to get close enough to see whether or not the shoes had red paint splattered across the toes.

"What are you doing?"

I whirled and came face-to-face with Susan. "Resting."

"What happened to your head?" She peered closer at the bump under my bangs.

"I, uh, fell. Yeah." I really was a horrible liar.

"That's what abused women say." She crossed her arms.

"Worried about me?" I raised my eyebrows, but that hurt, so I lost the smart-aleck look and smirked instead.

"If you're being abused, Kelly, you need to tell someone."

"Who on God's green earth would be abusing me?" It had been three years, four months, and fifteen days since I had a serious relationship with anyone other than Ruthie.

"Fine. Keep your secrets."

"Where's your photographer shadow?"

She shrugged. "I'm here to shop, not find news for my article. That would be time better spent on the studio lot. Not that anyone there will talk to me. It really does seem as if you'll win this crazy contest."

"I never took you for a quitter."

"Well, there is always a first time." She grinned. "You wouldn't be willing to share some of your information, would you?"

"Nope."

"I didn't think so." She glanced the way Tony had gone. "Why are you following that man?"

So, she didn't buy my story of resting. It was a lame explanation anyway. "I wanted to ask him about his shoes." There. I'd told the truth, so no stammering or sweating or getting red in the face.

"You really are a strange girl."

"That isn't the first time someone has called me strange."

"Have a nice day, Kelly, and try to stay on your feet." She strolled away from me and entered a women's clothing boutique.

That was a strange encounter. She'd actually seemed worried about me, and the fact she was seriously contemplating backing out of our competition left me worried. Could she have heard about the attack and wondered whether I would tell her the truth about it? If she had heard it was quite possible fear would make her drop out of writing about Lauren's death. I didn't blame her. If I wasn't so stubborn, I'd drop it all, too.

After twenty minutes of searching, I couldn't spot Tony again. I did manage to get some shots of celebrities coming in and out of shops, and one couple no one thought was a couple, seemed very intent on each other. That picture would sell better than the one of Ruthie and Doug, so the morning hadn't been a complete waste of time.

I stopped by an organic salad bar, ordered a

salad, and carried to an area of bistro-style tables in a brick courtyard. While I couldn't afford to shop in those particular shops, I loved the feel of the place. The classy, quiet richness of carefully placed plants and mood lighting.

"Good morning." The day got better as Brock sat down across from me with a veggie wrap in one hand and a bottle of water in the other. "How are you feeling? Should you be out and about?"

"I've got to pay the bills somehow."

"Didn't they pay you enough on the film to allow you to take it easy a bit?"

"I paid off my car." I stabbed a stubborn slice of tomato with my plastic fork. "I appreciate your concern, but I'm fine."

"Then why the crease between your eyes. You have a headache, don't you?"

"A little." I appreciated his concern, but it had been a very long time since someone actually cared. Oh, Ruthie loved me. I had no doubt, but she was pretty self-absorbed. Always had been, always would be. I loved her anyway.

His gaze rested on me for a while longer before he shook his head and ate his wrap. The frown on his face told me something weighed on his mind.

When I couldn't take the suspense anymore, I said, "Out with it. What's on your mind?"

Those amazing blue eyes rested on me and were filled with concern. "I like you, Kelly. A lot. When

I saw you lying on the floor of that bathroom, blood on your face…" He closed his eyes for a second before opening them again. "It scared me. I don't want you to continue finding out who killed Lauren."

I sat back. "Do you really think we haven't gone past the point of no return?"

"Last night was just a warning."

"The next time might not be."

I folded my arms. "I'm not stopping now. I want to find out what someone thinks I know."

"By getting killed in the process."

"I'll be fine." I tossed my napkin in my tray. "Thank you for your concern, Brock, but I'm a big girl and know what I'm doing." I headed for the trashcan.

He followed. "You're upset with me."

I took a deep breath and faced him. "No, I'm not, but I have to see this through. You asked for my help and Detective Lawrence has asked me to help her. People will talk to me."

"Law enforcement is having a civilian help in a murder investigation? Doesn't that seem strange to you?"

"Well, she did tell me to stay out of trouble while snooping…in so many words." I headed for the parking lot. This time he didn't follow, and I wished he had.

All four tires on my Volkswagon were flat.

From the long slit in each, it didn't take a genius to see they'd been cut. I fished my cell phone from my bag and called the police.

A squad car, followed by Detective Lawrence and Detective Sawyer, stopped next to my car fifteen minutes later. By now, Brock had realized I was still there and leaned against my baby blue car. He hadn't said a word, just given me a look that said, "I told you so".

Detective Lawrence waited stony-faced off to the side until the other officers had taken my statement and Detective Sawyer paced around the car a few times. When the uniformed officers left, she approached me. "First you're attacked, now your vehicle is vandalized. It's time for you to step back, Miss Canyon. We'll take it from here. I'd like you to hand over any notes you may have on this case."

"Thank you." Brock threw his hands in the air. "I told her the same thing half an hour ago. It's gotten too dangerous. When I asked her to help me clear my name, I had no idea things would get this bad."

Uh-oh. I hadn't told the detective Brock and I were kind of working together.

Lawrence cut me a sharp look, then returned her attention to Brock. "I never thought I'd hear myself agreeing with a movie star, but you're right. It's too dangerous."

"But my father—"

"Was a great detective," Sawyer interrupted, "one of the best, but you aren't a trained officer. I'm sure you have his instincts and I know for a fact he wouldn't want you in further danger."

"If you proceed with this investigation, Miss Canyon," Lawrence said, "I will have to arrest you for interfering."

"After you asked me to?"

"A very wrong decision on my part."

"Well, Detective," I said the words as sharp as I could. "I'll step back, for now, but if I get one more threat or one more act of violence toward me, then you will have to arrest me because I'll go forward with my snooping with everything in me. Brock, I need a ride home." Without waiting for any answers, I marched to his Jag and climbed into the leather interior.

Lawrence rapped her knuckles on the window.

With a sigh, I pushed the door open. "I can't open the window. Brock has the car keys."

"This will work. Please get out of the car, Miss Canyon."

I narrowed my eyes. "Why?"

"Have you ever spent the night in jail?"

"No. Again I'll ask why?"

"Because I think you need a taste of it." She unclipped handcuffs from her belt.

"You're arresting me?" I put my hands behind

my back and pressed them against the car.

"Are you resisting?"

Checkmate. Darn. "Fine. I won't do anymore snooping."

"I do not believe you."

I shrugged one shoulder. "You'll have to. I've done nothing wrong."

"Again, I cannot believe I'm saying this." She motioned Brock over. "I'm releasing this woman into your supervision. Since we are in agreement that she needs to stay out of my investigation, you are now her guard."

Brock grinned. The jerk!

"I will be very pleased to put her under lock and key."

I rolled my eyes. "Can I get back in the car now?"

"Yes." Lawrence gave me a thin-lipped smile and joined her partner next to their car.

"I'll call a tow truck," Brock said, sliding into the driver's seat. "I think I'm going to enjoy looking out for you."

"Shut up." I clicked my seatbelt in place. Ruthie was going to be over the moon about all this.

She was. She clapped her hands. "I'll make up the guest room right away." With the agility of a young woman, she bounded up the stairs.

"Can I trust you to stay safe for the thirty minutes it will take me to go home and get some things?" Brock asked.

"Considering that I'm a danger to myself, I don't see how you can possibly leave me for that long." I plopped onto the sofa, feeling every bit the sullen child I was acting like. I waved a dismissive hand at him. "Go. I'll be fine."

I would have to do my investigating during filming. All my suspects would be at the studio at one point. Detective Lawrence couldn't arrest me for going to work, right?

"What are you cooking up in that pretty head of yours?" Brock's gaze sharpened.

He called me pretty. Silly how much that simple phrase threatened to distract me. "Nothing. I'm tired." I laid my head back and closed my eyes. When I didn't hear the front door open and closed, I opened one eye to see Brock staring at me. "What?"

"You're a terrible liar." He turned and left, slamming the door behind him.

"Where did he go?" Ruthie carried an armload of bedding past me.

"To get some things."

"I'm in charge? Isn't that grand?" She laughed and headed back upstairs. The woman was like a ninja. I hadn't heard her come down.

I closed my eyes again and wondered whether I could convince my grandmother to help me make a prison break.

CHAPTER FIFTEEN

"**Oh, no you don't.**" Brock stood from his chair on the front patio. "I thought you might try sneaking away."

"I have work to do." I tried to squeeze past him only to find my way blocked as a muscular arm shot out and held me back.

"There's no filming until your knot is gone and taking pictures can wait a day or two."

"Fine." I whirled and headed back into the house.

Ruthie stepped from the kitchen, a pastry in one hand, and glared at me. "Hurry up and heal, would you? Do you know how hard it is to act with nothing but a green screen behind you and a stand in?"

"No, I don't know, but I imagine it would be difficult." I fell onto the sofa and grabbed one of Lauren's photo albums. If I was going to be stuck in the house all day, maybe I'd find something I'd missed before. "I don't like being idle, Ruthie."

"I know, sweetie. I'm being a harpy. We're filming an important scene…the one where you go missing." She smiled. "Shouldn't be too hard, should it? But it is. I'm not that worried about some stand-in being kidnapped. It's a real test of my acting ability. Things are very different than they used to be." She grabbed her purse. "Do have a good day with Brock." She gave me a wink on her way out the door.

I groaned and opened the album. After half an hour, I decided looking at pictures was a waste of time. Been there, done that. I needed to be at the studio asking questions. I needed to be looking for a pair of white shoes with red paint splatters.

"Coffee?" Brock entered the house and made a beeline for the kitchen.

"Yes," I called after him. When he returned and handed me a mug, I asked, "Can we go to the studio today and look at people's shoes?"

He peered at me over the rim of his cup. "Do you actually think they'd be wearing the very shoes they wore to paint your porch?"

I shrugged. "They wore them when they attacked me at the fundraiser. While I can't really picture Louie or Doug wearing those type of shoes, we don't know what they wear at home. It's possible. I saw Tony in a pair, Marilyn goes to the gym, so it's feasible she has a pair…"

"I'm not sure we'll find out anything, but let's go." He took my mug and set it on the table. "We can stop at the coffee shop on the way and get you something chocolate."

"Don't try to butter me up. I'm still mad that I'm virtually a prisoner." I grabbed my camera bag and over-sized shoulder bag and marched out the front door.

"You aren't a prisoner," Brock said, hurrying to catch up. "You're under my protection."

"Prisoner." I got into his car and slammed the door.

"You really are the most stubborn person I've ever met." He turned the key in the ignition. "Do me a favor, will you?"

"What?" I cut him a sideways glance.

"Don't run off when we get to the studio. We'll go wherever you want, but I go with you."

"That works for me." I turned my head and smiled. He'd be easy enough to give the slip to if I really wanted to. Which I didn't. I was just vain enough to like the envious glances sent my way from women who saw us together.

Brock parked close to the studio gates, a perk of being a big star, and rushed to open my door before I could. "You never let me be the gentleman."

"I'm not used to it." I offered him my hand.

Not letting go, he helped me from the car and held on as we strolled across the lot. I puffed up like a peacock, my smile not fading until we entered the studio and Louie glared our way.

"What are you doing here?" he shouted. "You're injured."

"I'm fine. Even though you don't think Amber can work miracles at covering up my bump, I thought I should be here to watch and keep up on things." I grinned.

"I could totally cover that." Amber flipped my bangs over my forehead as she passed.

"Fine. Tomorrow, you start filming." Louie turned back to the actors. "Take twelve. Ruthie, your daughter has just been kidnapped. Act like it."

"Brock, look." I motioned to Tony and his white shoes.

"Hmm. Maybe you should stand opposite your grandmother. She really seems to be struggling."

I shook my head and moved closer to Tony. "Nice shoes." They were spotless. "Do you have another pair?"

He glanced up from behind his camera. "An older pair at home, why?"

"Just wondering."

"Canyon!" Louie narrowed his eyes. "If you're going to distract people, then come stand over here so Ruthie can look at you. Nevermind. Lunch break. Amber, cover up Canyon's bump. She's working today." Clipboard under his arm, Louie stormed off set.

"Lunch?" Ruthie glanced at the clock. "It's only nine a.m."

"It's your fault," David James said. "If you hadn't messed up twenty times—"

"Eleven." High spots of color appeared on Ruthie's cheeks. "Actors have had more takes than that before."

"Come on." Brock took Ruthie by the elbow. "Let's get to the trailer before you throw a punch at his face."

"I'd like to." She cuddled up to his arm, leaving me to trail behind.

I didn't care. I studied everyone's shoes that we passed.

"I lost one job to Lauren, I won't lose one to you." A woman's voice shrieked from behind a trailer.

Seeing that Brock was engrossed in whatever Ruthie was saying, I ducked back and peeked to see who sounded like a banshee. Iris Beacon, a towel wrapped around her head and stage makeup caked on her face bent close to Marilyn Carter and jabbed a finger in the other woman's chest.

"Got it?"

Marilyn slapped her hand away. "I'm not after your part. I'm talented enough not to resort to stealing."

"Ha! You're no different than Lauren."

"Take that back."

"I won't." Iris straightened. "The truth hurts doesn't it?"

"You are going to be one sorry woman if you interfere with the casting on the movie."

"Not as sorry as you'll be if you get the part I want." Iris yanked open the door to the trailer they stood by and slammed it behind her.

These people took acting very seriously. Almost as serious as I was at being determined to beat Susan out of the article on Lauren's death. I turned and smacked into Brock.

"I told you not to leave me," he said.

"Technically, you walked off and left me." I smiled up at him. "Is Amber ready for me?"

"She's been ready." He motioned his head toward the trailer.

"Wonderful." I patted his cheek. "If you're a good boy, I'll tell you what I overheard later."

He made a noise deep in his throat. "Ruthie can get away with that type of behavior, but you can't."

"What kind of behavior can I get away with?"

His eyes darkened. "If you aren't careful, you're bound to find out. Has anyone ever kissed you breathless before?"

"Oh." I dashed up the steps and into the trailer.

Once I sat down, Amber frowned at my forehead. "You got this at the fundraiser? Must have been one heck of a party."

"You're right on that." I tilted my face up and

let her do her magic. By the time she'd caked on enough makeup for ten people and covered the lovely blue and purple of my bump, she styled my hair so that my bangs fell forward and finished the job of obscuring all sights of my mishap.

"You are a genius." Ruthie clapped her hands. "You can't even tell."

"You need to be more careful about walking into doors, Kelly. You might not be as lucky next time."

"I didn't walk into a door." I studied her reaction.

She paled. "Oh. I, uh, that's what I heard."

"What exactly did you hear?"

"That you walked into a door." She turned around and busied herself with the various bottles and jars on the table. "You could get a concussion doing that."

I twisted my mouth. "Who told you what happened?"

"I'm not sure. I think I overheard some of the cafeteria staff talking. A few of them catered the dinner, I think."

I stood and removed the apron she always placed around my neck. "The fundraiser had nothing to do with the studio. I doubt any of the staff from here were there."

"Kelly's right," Brock said, crossing his arms. "So, where did you hear what happened?"

"Fine. I was there, okay?" She whirled around, her face red. "I never get invited to those fancy parties, so I snuck in the back door. I saw the paramedics arrive and I saw them leave. Happy?"

"Why didn't you say so?" I shook my head. "There was no need to lie. You wouldn't be the first person to sneak in somewhere."

Tears welled in her eyes. "I guess my pride got the better of me. I've always wanted what the rest of you have, what Lauren had, but I can't get my lucky break."

"You want to be an actor?" I folded the apron and set it on the chair. "Do you have a manager?"

"No."

"I'm sure Ruthie can get you an appointment with Doug."

"Really?" Hope sprang in her eyes. "I asked Lauren many times, but she refused. She said I didn't look like a star."

"Stars come in all shapes and sizes," Ruthie said, giving her a hug. "I'll see what I can do, but any auditions are on you."

"Oh, I can act." She grinned and swiped her hand across her eyes. "I'm very grateful. You'd better get back to the set. We've taken longer than Louie allowed."

I thought about the conversation between Iris and Marilyn, and ours with Amber, as Brock, Ruthie, and I headed back to the set. Iris just became another suspect. "We have more suspects than we do answers." I told the other two what I'd overheard. "Does Iris strike you as a murderer?"

"Anyone can kill under the right circumstances," Brock said.

CHAPTER SIXTEEN

Today was Amber's big day. The day of her audition for a small role in an upcoming sitcom. She seemed surprised when Ruthie offered that her and I go along for support, but agreed with a strained smile. So, here we sat, in chairs at the back of a room behind three people at a table.

On the other side of the room, Marilyn filed her nails, looking bored. Supposedly she was there for an audition of her own and refused to sit in the waiting room like everyone else. Stardom had its perks.

Amber was number twenty of thirty people hoping to be the sister of the main character. She stepped confidently in front of the table and read her lines, doing her best to act as if her feelings were hurt by something one of those at the table read. When she'd finished, she turned to leave.

"Now, we have makeup people wanting to act?" Marilyn stood and tossed a patronizing look toward the table. "First paparazzi, now makeup. Everyone wants a piece of the pie. Amber, sweetie, give it up before someone shoots you down." With those words, she sailed from the room.

"That's all, Miss Jacobson. Someone will contact your manager." The woman sitting between two men stared at the door Marilyn had exited. "Where did she go? It's her turn."

Dismissed, Amber's face fell. She cast a wide-eyed glance at me and Ruthie before darting from the room.

Ruthie paused in front of the table. "Amber was the best we've seen today. Don't let the jealous words of a bitter woman ruin her chances." She put her nose in the air and gracefully strolled out, leaving me to follow.

We headed for the trailer where Amber had collapsed on the sofa in tears. "I hate that woman. I hate all these movie stars."

Ruthie's eyes widened. "Don't lump us all together, dear." She sat next to the other woman and patted her back. "You did fine. Any producer worth their salt won't listen to someone like Marilyn."

"But she's an A-lister," Amber wailed.

"So what. Now, chin up and go wash your face. I have a scene to film."

"Alright." She shuffled down the hall with slumped shoulders, but when she reached the bathroom, she squared her shoulders and her eyes hardened. "After all, I'm nothing more than a makeup person, right?"

Ruthie glanced at me. "That is her current job, am I wrong?"

"No, you aren't wrong." I propped my feet on the coffee table. I had a scene to film later in the day with Ruthie and the man playing my father. I could wait until Ruthie had finished and spend some time thinking over this twisted web surrounding Lauren's death.

What I really wanted to do was wander the lot and question the workers. More than one person had told me they saw and heard more than anyone. Someone had to know something. The problem was…they most likely didn't know they knew something. It would take asking the right questions of the right person. And, I couldn't go anywhere without my guard dog and he hadn't shown up yet.

"Good morning." Speaking of the handsome devil, Brock entered the trailer. "I picked up your car, Kelly."

"Thank you. Now, let's go." I jumped to my feet with promises to return in time for my makeup. Grabbing Brock's hand, I pulled him outside after me. "I want to question some people. Who worked the night of the award's party? No matter how insignificant the job?"

He rubbed his chin. "Hmm. Amber was there doing Lauren's makeup, of course. Doug, some caterers…as for workers from the studio…I'm not sure, but I know who might. Come on."

Brock led me to the maintenance shed where Rod Looper and Ben Jones sat smoking outside. "Got a minute?"

Rod nodded. "Sure. We got ten minutes left on our break. What's up?"

"Kelly has some more questions about the night Lauren died."

He turned his attention to me. "You aren't going to quote names in that article, are you? Because it might get some of us fired."

"No, I'll leave names out." Brock unfolded a chair for me and I sat facing the two other men. "Were you working that night?"

"Yep. We both were, although the party was almost over when we arrived. If we get an opportunity to make some extra cash, we do. Someone had to clean up."

"Who else from here worked that night?"

He glanced at Ben. "Mary was there, right?"

"Yep. A couple of the younger ladies who work the cafeteria helped cater. Lisa and Roberta, I think. Oh, and that golf cart driver was there. Not sure why since most folks showed up in limos."

I made a mental note to talk to Frank and the two caterers. "Who catered the event?"

"Leo's," Ben said. "They cater all the big shindigs."

"Thank you. I've got to get made up but if you remember anything that might help me, please call me." I pulled a business card from my pocket. "No matter how insignificant it might seem."

"Heard you got slammed in the bathroom at the fundraiser." Rod slipped the card into his shirt pocket. "If you're going to keep asking questions, you're going to have to expect someone coming after you."

"Are you threatening me?"

"Heck no." He shook his head. "Just alerting you to the fact that folks around here will do anything to get top billing."

"Does either of you have a pair of white canvas shoes?" It wasn't a stretch to guess they had access to paint.

They shared a glance, then in unison said, "no."

"But all the cafeteria staff wear them," Ben said. "Why? That's kind of an odd question."

"Just wondering." I smiled. "Thanks." As Brock and I headed back to the trailer, I said, "we need to talk to the cafeteria staff and the staff at Leo's."

He groaned. "You're going to get us both killed."

It was almost quitting time when Brock and

I were able to make our way to the cafeteria. After a few questions as to who Lisa and Roberta were, we were directed to the staff lounge. When asked if we could ask some questions, Lisa frowned, "I don't like to stay late."

"I'll pay you each fifty dollars to stay," Brock said, motioning to a round table with four chairs. "Just for a few minutes, please."

They both took a seat. Brock and I sat across from them.

I went through my spiel about writing an article in regard to Lauren's murder. "I was told you both worked that night."

"Horrible thing," Roberta said. "Yes, we were there. I carried a tray with flutes of champagne. Lisa carried wine. Miss Mayfield had a lot of wine."

"Did either of you see who came and went from her dressing room?"

"I did," Lisa said. "I brought the wine straight to her. Her makeup artist was in and out all night. Mr. Hanson was, too. Her manager, that actor, Gary Porter, a janitor—"

"Janitor?" I glanced at Brock. "Why would a janitor be there during the festivities?"

"I didn't see his face," Lisa continued, "but he wore navy coveralls and a baseball cap. He was fat and short."

Finally, we were getting somewhere. Ben Jones was on the short and hefty scale. He'd also admitted to being there. He could have arrived earlier than we thought. "Anything else?"

She shrugged. "I'm sure there were others. I didn't camp outside her room, and there was a lot of people there that night."

"I understand." I handed them both a business card. "Please call me if you think of anything at all."

Roberta stared at the card for a minute. "I didn't see the janitor, but I did smell a perfume that didn't belong to Miss Mayfield."

"How do you know that?" Brock's eyes narrowed.

"Because I like what she wore and tried to buy some. Way out of my price range. What I smelled when I looked into the room during all the commotion was a lot sweeter. Almost sicky sweet. Something I've smelled at the drugstore."

Amber wore a sweet cologne, but she had a reason to be there. Now, not only would I be looking at everyone's shoes, I'd be sniffing them. I stood and waited while Brock handed each of the women a fifty-dollar bill.

Outside, I said, "We need to talk to Ben Jones. He fits the description of the person Lisa saw going into Lauren's room."

"I agree." We returned to the maintenance shed to find out Rod and Ben had left for the day.

"What kind of perfume did Lauren wear?" I

asked.

"Gypsy something. It's not that expensive. Around fifty dollars."

I rolled my eyes. "That's a lot of money for someone who makes minimum wage, Brock. Stop being a snob."

"I'm not a snob." He frowned. "Am I?"

"You tend to be." By now we had reached my car and I slid into the driver's seat.

Brock got in the other side. "I never would have thought of myself that way. What's wrong with enjoying the fruits of my labors? I make a lot of money. I like nice things."

"There's nothing wrong with that, just don't expect others to be able to afford the same things." I turned the key in the ignition and drove from the parking lot. "I'm hungry. Since you have so much money you can buy dinner."

He glanced at my faded jeans, mussed hair, and heavy makeup. "Burgers it is."

"There you go, being a snob again."

"How so? Do you really want to go somewhere nice looking like that?"

I laughed. "Not really. Let's get the burgers to go and head to the park. Maybe we can do some brainstorming."

Twenty minutes later we sat at a picnic table overlooking a fountain as the sun settled over the city. I tried to concentrate on what we'd learned that day, but having Brock sit across from me in such a romantic setting kept pulling my mind away from the task at hand. If I wasn't eating a burger with onions, I'd have kissed him.

CHAPTER SEVENTEEN

Another day of filming, another day of asking questions with no solid answers, another day without a kiss from Brock. I was in a sorry state for sure. I lay on my bed, fully dressed after a day of work and thought of kisses instead of the investigation into Lauren's murder. Sighing, I swung my legs over the side of the bed and got to my feet.

"Brock's here," Ruthie sang skipping past my room. "He's taking us for pizza. Get up. Don't keep him waiting.

"I'm coming." I took a quick glance in the mirror and noticed I still wore thick makeup. I rushed to the bathroom, washed my face, tucked my hair up under a denim cap blinged out with rhinestones, and still beat Ruthie to the livingroom. "Hello, Brock."

"Hey, Kelly." He gave me a lazy grin. "You are the cutest girl in the world and I bet you don't even try."

My face flushed. Cute, pretty, beautiful…I rarely heard those words from a handsome man. Of course, I was snapping photos of most men until they grew annoyed and shooed me away. "Uh, thanks."

"I'm ready." Ruthie skipped down the stairs and slipped her arm in Brock's. "I'm starving."

"Bad enough that you'll eat a whole slice?" I laughed and opened the front door.

"It's quite possible I might risk gaining a pound, so yes, I'm that hungry." She stuck her nose in the air and sailed outside ahead of us.

A horn honked as it passed driving too fast for our residential street. I glared at the speeding Cadillac convertible.

"That Marilyn always was a speed demon." Ruthie waved, then slid into the front passenger seat leaving me to climb in the back. "She's going to get into an accident one of these days."

"She grew up around race tracks," Brock said, turning the key in the ignition. "She's quite a skilled driver."

Ruthie didn't look convinced as she peered into the mirror on the back of the visor and applied lipstick the color of cotton candy. She pursed, smacked, then flipped the visor back up. "I hope you're right. While we aren't what you'd call friends, we are polite to each other."

Which to Ruthie meant a lot. I smiled at the back of her head and clicked my seatbelt into place.

We drove up the coast to a small hole-in-the-wall pizza parlor that had the world's best pizza despite no advertising other than word-of-mouth. Celebrity watchers could almost always spot a star in the dark recesses of the pizza parlor. Today was no exception.

We entered and tossed smiles toward Louie and Marie. "Sure is strange that they are together more now that they're divorcing than before," Ruthie said.

"The pressure to please is gone," Brock said, holding up three fingers to the hostess. "They can enjoy each other's company again without worrying about irritating their spouse somehow."

I tilted my head. "You don't seem like a fan of marriage."

"I'm a definite fan." He grinned. "My parents have been married sixty years and live on a small farm in the Ozarks. They have been a great example for me. I hope to have what they have someday…a good marriage, a chunk of land, regular church attendance, and a laid back life. I've done my best to live by the morals they taught me."

Sounded wonderful. I wondered whether he'd be able to walk away from fame and fortune in Hollywood. My father had, even though we'd stayed in Los Angeles. Brock did seem to be one of the last good guys in tinsel town.

The hostess led us to a circular booth in the far corner of the restaurant. Marilyn sat at a small table with a dark-haired man. Neither of them looked happy. In fact, they looked as if either of them could shoot flames from their nostrils. "Who's that man with Marilyn?"

"Leo Staletti," Ruthie said. "He's the most sought-after caterer around."

"The same Leo that catered the award dinner?"

Brock nodded. "The very same. Marilyn must be wanting him to cater something for her. He owns this pizzeria, in addition to a more upscale Italian restaurant. His prices are high and the food excellent."

Marilyn threw a wadded-up napkin at Leo's face and stormed out of the restaurant via a swinging back door. He followed a mere second later.

"That doesn't seem like an argument between customer and caterer." Ruthie's eyes widened. "That seems more like a lover's spat."

I agreed. The wounded expressions on their faces did seem more personal than someone upset over high prices. Could it be possible that Marilyn was seeing not only Louie but Leo?

Raised voices pulled Brock from his seat. "Let me go make sure they aren't getting physical. Order a large meat lovers, please." He marched through the same door the other two had gone out of.

As the door would swing to and fro, I'd occasionally hear the low rumble of his voice as he tried to placate the other two. Ruthie placed the pizza order when the waitress returned with glasses of ice water and a bottle of wine, on the house, the waitress said.

A few minutes later, Brock re-entered with Louie as tires screeched from the parking lot.

Leo said something to Brock, then pulled a set of keys from his pocket before heading back through the swinging doors. Brock shrugged and slid into the booth next to me. "It's definitely a lover's spat. Problem is, Leo had no idea Marilyn was also seeing Louie. She chose tonight to tell him she was pregnant and getting a DNA test to see which of them was the father."

"Stupid woman." Ruthie shook her head. "Neither needed to know. She could just have the baby and go on with her life. People do it all the time."

"That doesn't make it right, grandma." I frowned. "There's too many love triangles in this town."

"I agree," she said. "I don't live that way, neither does Brock. You're just seeing the worst of the worst lately. Your father was a good man despite his stardom, so is Brock. They aren't all like Marilyn, Lauren, and Louie."

"Good to know."

"You're just used to taking photos of people coming and going and not really getting to know any of them."

Brock laid his arm along the back of the booth. "I told myself when I entered into this business I'd do my best to be the man my parents raised."

Ruthie reached across the table and patted his free hand. "You've done a fine job."

I wanted to concentrate on the conversation about the ills of living in Hollywood and the struggle it was to stay a good person, but the tips of Brock's fingers brushed my shoulder and sent shivers up and down my spine. Not the kind you got from being skittish, but the kind you got when you were very aware of the man sitting next to you wearing a musky cologne that sent every sense into overdrive.

The pizza arrived, and my attention turned to eating as Brock withdrew his arm. I could breathe again.

Louie returned half-way through our dinner and paused next to our table. "Pizza's on the house. Thank you, Hanson for helping me see reason," He glanced from Ruthie to me, then shuffled away.

"What did you tell him?" I asked.

"That a woman like Marilyn wasn't worth the heartache." Brock shrugged. "I think he really cared for her."

"Poor man," Ruthie said, glancing over her shoulder. "Maybe I should console him. He's more my age than hers anyway."

"Leave him be," Brock said. "At least for a few weeks. Sometimes, even a man needs to mourn a broken heart."

After we finished off the pizza, Ruthie eating two slices and having two glasses of wine, we left and headed down the coast for home. We'd gone maybe five miles before I straightened in my seat. "Pull over."

"Why?" Brock glanced in the rearview mirror.

"I see something." I prayed I hadn't seen what I thought I had.

Brock pulled onto the shoulder of the road, coming dangerously close to the edge of a cliff. "Be careful," he called as I shoved open my door.

I swayed a moment but caught my footing and moved to where the ground sloped a little more gently toward the ocean.

My heart lodged in my throat. I had seen what I thought I had. The rear lights of a vehicle stuck wrong end up through some shrubs. "Brock!"

He slid on loose rocks in his hurry to get to me.

I pointed.

"Oh, no." He bent and slid toward the car. "It's Marilyn! Have Ruthie call 9-1-1."

"Got it." I hadn't seen her get out of the car. Since she wore heels, she wisely chose to stay on the blacktop and pushed numbers on her cell phone.

I slid down to join Brock, grabbing hold of the edge of the car window to slow my descent. After a few frightening slips toward the edge, I found my footing.

Marilyn sat hunched over the steering wheel. Blood from a gash in her head covered her face.

I reached over and felt for a pulse. "She's alive."

"Thank God." Brock opened the passenger side door.

I screamed as the car moved a few inches. I glanced at the beach about fifty feet below us. "We've got to get her out of there before we all get dragged over."

"Unhook her seatbelt, then get back." Brock put one knee on the passenger seat. When the car didn't move, he pulled in his other knee and reached for Marilyn.

I stretched my arm and pressed the seatbelt release, then jumped for a bush growing on the side of the cliff as the car shifted again. "Hurry, Brock."

Sirens wailed in the distance. I didn't think they'd reach us in time.

Brock grabbed Marilyn's arm as I dangled like a monkey in a tree. He moved backward, slow inch by slow inch until he could get his arms under both of hers. Then he planted his feet on the ground, fell backward, and rolled as the car went over the side.

"Brock!"

"I'm alright." He waved an arm. "A little bruised, but still breathing. So is Marilyn. I do think I'll lay here until help arrives though."

Using shrubs to keep me from joining the car, I made my way to his side. His leg bled from a stick protruding through his calf and jeans. He couldn't have moved if he wanted to. I unwound the scarf around Marilyn's hair and tied a tourniquet just above the knee before making sure the other woman did indeed still breathe.

Using the hem of her dress, I pulled it up and dabbed at the wound on her head. The blood had started to clot.

"You okay down there?" Ruthie's voice drifted on the breeze. "Want me to come down there?"

"No, thanks. Just direct the paramedics when they get here."

"Will do, dear."

"You're a hero," I told Brock, leaning back against a rock that I hoped was secure enough to hold me. "There's no way I could have gotten her out without you."

"You're the one who noticed the car in the front place. If not for you, she'd be dead." He groaned and shifted Marilyn in his arms. "It's amazing how heavy an unconscious woman is."

A camera flashed above us. Ruthie waved. "I thought this would make a good picture for the front of one of the papers."

She was right. Snapping photos of a mega-movie star saving the life of another would definitely sell papers.

I locked my gaze on the descending paramedics and waited.

CHAPTER EIGHTEEN

It was nearing midnight by the time we got home and got Brock, complete with a cast on his leg, settled into the guestroom. After pain meds, it didn't take long for him to fall sleep.

Although I was exhausted beyond belief, I sat in the plush arm chair next to the bed and pondered on how absolutely wrong I was about Brock upon first meeting him. I'd thought him shallow and arrogant—a pre-conceived idea of Hollywood stars. This wonderful man had risked his life for another without a second thought.

I must have fallen asleep because the next thing I knew Ruthie was shaking me and sun streamed through the bedroom window. I groaned and straightened from the slouch I'd spent the last few hours in.

"Go to bed, sweetie. I'll watch Brock." She set a bell on the nightstand. "He can ring this, and I'll come running."

"I didn't mean to fall asleep." In fact, Brock didn't need twenty-four watching. He wasn't in any danger of dying. "I just meant to sit and let the day's stress melt away then go to bed."

"Did it work?"

"Not really." I shuffled past her and headed to my room.

"Kelly."

I bolted to a sitting position at the sound of Brock's voice. "What are you doing out of bed?"

"Detectives Lawrence and Sawyer are here and they want to talk to us."

"Now?" I shoved tangled hair away from my face.

"Yep." He turned and thumped away on crutches.

Cruel, that's what the detectives were. Making a cripple, albeit a temporary one, and an exhausted woman come at their beck and call. I shoved a baseball cap on my uncombed hair and stomped downstairs.

"Couldn't this have waited?" I plopped onto the sofa next to Brock and Ruthie. "We've been through trauma."

"Not really." Detective Lawrence sat in a chair opposite us and motioned for Sawyer to take the other matching chair. "I'm hoping you can tell us who might have wanted Marilyn dead?"

"She died?" My throat clogged.

"No, she's in a coma." Lawrence held up a hand. "But, someone wanted her dead. Her brakes had been cut."

I glanced at Brock, then back at the detective. "I know of several people unhappy with her. Louie and Marie Stock, Amber Jacobson, and Leo Staletti." I explained my reasons, mentioning Leo might have been the last one to see Marilyn before she'd sped off.

Lawrence pursed her lips and wrote something on a small notepad before looking back up. "No more questioning people. We'll take it from here." She stood and pierced me with a sharp glance. "I appreciate your help, but it's gotten too dangerous, even for Detective Canyon's daughter."

I doubted I could stop now. I was in too deep, but I nodded as Ruthie stood to let them out. Once they were out of earshot, I said, "It's too late for me to stop now. Especially after the threats I've gotten."

"I agree, but I also follow the detective's reasoning." Brock propped his cast on the coffee table. "That could as easily have been you over that cliff, Kelly."

"True. I think we've narrowed our suspect list down to the names I gave Lawrence."

He frowned. "Are you even listening to anyone's advice?"

"I'm hearing every word and choosing to

disregard." I crossed my arms and sat back. "Not only have I been threatened, but don't forget the competition with Susan. I'm determined to win."

"At the risk of your life?"

"If that's what it takes to get me a good reporting job, yes."

He groaned. "Can't you stick to acting or paparazzi? It's a lot safer."

I sighed. "I'll fix breakfast. Do you need a pill?"

"No. I hate those things."

I pushed to my feet and headed for the kitchen. Brock was right. I had my teeth set so hard on becoming a reporter I wasn't thinking straight. I'd never become a reporter if I was dead. I gripped the counter. Maybe I should step back and let the authorities solve Lauren's murder and let Susan win the front-page article.

I couldn't. I wasn't a quitter.

I fried some bacon, scrambled some eggs, and made coffee before shaking Brock awake. Ruthie wasn't in sight, but the sound of water running through the pipes told me where she was. "Time to eat, Sleeping Beauty."

He cracked open one eye. "I'd rather sleep."

"You can go back to bed after." I held out one hand and grabbed a crutch with the other. Soon, Brock was thudding along behind me on the way to the kitchen.

"I've been thinking," Ruthie said, coming in

behind us. "Who could have had access to Marilyn's brake lines?"

"Everyone I named to the detectives." I set a plate in front of Brock.

"Not Leo. He wouldn't have had time."

I blinked a few times. She was right. Leo was in our sight most of the time. "Ruthie, you're a genius. That knocks four suspects down to three. Tell me we're filming today."

"We are." She grinned. "At least two of those three will be there. If Marie isn't, we'll hunt her down."

"You two are insane." Brock dug his fork into his eggs. "I hope you'll let me wash up first."

"You are staying here," I said. "You're in no condition to go anywhere for a day or two."

He scowled. "I've been on crutches before."

"Tell me your leg isn't killing you."

"That would be a lie."

I grinned. "So, that means you will stay here. Ruthie and I are quite capable of questioning our suspects and not putting ourselves in danger."

"Ha." He slammed his fork down. "You are the most stubborn woman I've ever met in my life."

"She takes after me, darling." Ruthie patted his arm. "We'll be fine. I've got pepper spray and a big knife in my purse."

Brock rolled his eyes. "Both of which require you to get up close and personal."

"My favorite place to be." She kissed his cheek. "Eat up, Kelly. We've got to be at makeup in half an hour."

We weren't the only ones late. By the time we arrived at the trailer, Amber was sprinting across the lot toward us. "Sorry, sorry." She yanked open the trailer door and ushered us inside. "I overslept." She eyed a scratch on my cheek. "What happened to you? Can't you keep from damaging your face? It takes me longer to cover up scratches, bumps and bruises."

"My apologies." I rolled my eyes. As if I'd asked to be attacked or skid down a hill to help rescue someone. Being a Good Samaritan obviously had its downside.

By the time Amber worked her magic, you couldn't tell I'd had a scratch on my face. I could barely smile or talk with so much makeup on, but at least I looked good.

Louie shook his head at me when I waltzed in. "No closeups on Canyon today," he told Tony. "She looks like a mannequin."

There went my self-esteem. Lucky for all involved, we were shooting an action scene where I escaped a dark basement to get away from my crazed movie father. With all my aches and pains from the evening before, filming was difficult and frustrating for everyone.

"Cut!" Louie threw down his clipboard. "We'll

try again tomorrow." He stormed from the set.

"Wait." I tried to run toward him, but it was more like a shuffling lurch. "I'm sure you've heard of Marilyn's accident."

"Yeah, so?" He stopped and turned. "Don't tell me you were one of the rescuers."

"I was. I'm sore and tired. I promise I'll be better tomorrow."

He grabbed me for a hug. "You are a saint!" He held me back and kissed my forehead.

"Oh. Uh. Do you mind telling me where you were last night between the hours of six and ten and whether you have a viable alibi?"

He laughed. "Sweetheart, I was home alone drunk off my rear end. My wife wants a divorce, one of my girlfriends is dead, and the other in a coma. It has not been a good week, so I thought I'd drown my cares." He patted me on the top of my head as if I were a dog and left me standing there.

I couldn't believe his excuses for having a bad week. All they did was show what kind of a low-down skunk he was. I almost hoped he was the killer so he could be put behind bars for the rest of his life.

I left the studio and stood in the middle of the lot, my face raised to the sun. Someone cleared their voice behind me. Ugh. Susan.

"Well, well, what you won't do to make the front page," she said.

"You mean save a life?" I turned and grinned. "Jealous?"

"Hardly." A tic developed next to her right eye. "I've got enough information to finish my story. Do you?"

"You know the identity of Lauren's killer?" My eyebrows rose despite the glue on my face.

"Of course not. Do you?"

"I've got suspects."

She frowned. "You can't falsely accuse someone in the press, Kelly."

"I'm not an idiot, Susan. I'll make sure an arrest has been made before I write anything."

She stared intently at me. "You're serious?"

"Yes."

"You're actually trying to solve the murder?"

I crossed my arms. "Aren't you?"

"No, I was focusing on Lauren's character. I'm not a cop." She narrowed her eyes. "Neither are you. This could be dangerous, Kelly."

"It's sweet that you're worried about me, but I'll be fine." I flashed her a smile and headed for the trailer.

Neither Amber or Ruthie were in the trailer which meant I had a few minutes to snoop around and see if I'd missed anything regarding Lauren and who might have wanted to kill her. I headed for the bedroom and opened the closet. A few evening gowns hung there, obviously ones Amber had wanted to keep. I had just reached for a box on the shelf when I heard the front door open.

I closed the door and made a painful dash for the bathroom. I'd just closed the door when someone knocked. "Hold on. I'll be out in a minute."

"It's just me," Amber said. "I wasn't expecting you to be here so soon."

"Filming was canceled," I sang out, flushing the toilet and turning on the faucet. After a few more seconds, I exited coming to a stop at the sight of a dressed-up Amber. "What have you been up to?"

She grinned. "I got called for a second audition. It seems that witch, Marilyn, might not have ruined my chances after all."

"You do know that 'witch' is lying in a coma, don't you?"

She put a hand to her mouth. "What? No."

For some reason I didn't think she was as upset as she tried to act. I narrowed my eyes, then pushed past her. I fished some makeup remover towelettes from a box and started scrubbing my face. Louie, Marie, Amber, their names whirled in my head. One of them was a killer, and I intended to find out which one.

I tossed the towelette in a nearby trashcan and glanced up to see Amber watching me with a hard glint in her eyes. I met her stare until she looked away. What was going on in her little mind? I started to ask if she had a problem with me, but changed my mind when Ruthie joined us.

She glanced from me to Amber, then sent me a questioning look. I shrugged and tossed her the box of makeup removers. I could tell Ruthie had something she wanted to tell me, something important.

CHAPTER NINETEEN

On the drive home, I turned to Ruthie. "Spill it."

"I thought you'd never ask." She pulled a brown sack from her shoulder bag. "I found the white sneakers."

"What?" I turned to her so fast I almost ran off the road.

"Red paint and all. The best part is our killer is a woman or a man with very small feet." She pulled them from the bag and held them up.

"Where did you find them?"

"In a dumpster behind the studio."

I was almost afraid to ask. "What were you doing behind the studio?"

"Kissing Doug." She wiggled her eyebrows. "It's more private back there. Unless you're a smoker, no one goes back there. I spotted the shoes and waited for Doug to go back to his office, then I grabbed them. They are a size eight and a half," she said with a flourish as she dropped them back in her bag.

Amber and Marie most likely wore that size. Possibly Marilyn, too. Although she'd been run off the road, I hadn't completely erased her from my suspect list. Her accident could be something other than related to Lauren's murder. That gave us three suspects, letting Louie off the hook in regard to Lauren, at least.

"We'll have to turn them in to the police. Set them on the dash and take pictures from every angle, even the bottom."

"Oh, this is fun." She set the shoes on the dash and pulled out her cell phone, snapping pictures until we pulled into the precinct parking lot.

Catching sight of Lawrence heading into the building, I laid on the horn. She turned and I waved her over. She clearly wasn't pleased to be summoned that way.

I rolled down the driver side window and smiled. "We have a gift for you."

Ruthie handed her the shoes.

Lawrence narrowed her eyes. "Where did you get these?"

"Behind the studio."

"I thought I told you to back off."

I shrugged. "I wasn't the one to find them. Ruthie was doing a make-out session with her manager."

"Too much information." She shuddered. "I wish you two hadn't touched them."

Ruthie raised her hand. "I'm the only one who touched them. I'll be glad to give you my fingerprints…oh, wait, they're in the system. About ten years ago, I had this little episode with a rival actress…" she waved a dismissive hand. "Let's just say the jails need some updating to make them more comfortable."

Lawrence stared impassively for a moment. "You make me want to shoot myself." Shoes in hand, she marched into the building.

"Let's go tell Brock what we found." I turned the car toward home. Things were stepping up. I'd find out what size shoe the three women wore and go from there. Which wouldn't be hard in Marilyn's case. "Changed my mind. Let's see if Marilyn is awake." I made a U-turn and headed for the hospital.

"Yes, she's awake, but only family is permitted in ICU," the nurse said.

"I'm her aunt. I'm Ruthie Canyon, the—"

The nurse glanced up. "I know you! I've seen all of your movies. I had no idea you were related to Miss Carter. Please, go on back." She smiled. "But only for fifteen minutes."

We hurried down the hall before Ruthie's fan could change her mind and entered Marilyn's dark room. The television was on, but the volume low. She turned her head.

Her head was wrapped in a bandage, one leg in a cast and in traction. "Thank you, Kelly, for saving me."

"Thank Brock. He's the one who pulled you from the car." I sat in one of the stuffed chairs. It obviously paid to be a celebrity.

"I plan to. I heard he was injured." She closed her eyes.

"Can you tell us what happened?" I glanced around the room for a pair of shoes. Nothing. The room was clean, but a small closet sat against one wall.

"I'd left the restaurant a bit upset. I was going too fast around that curve, but when I went to slow down, the brake pedal went all the way to the floor. I pumped it a few times, but the car wouldn't slow. The last thing I knew I woke up here with the news that you and Brock saved my life."

Ruthie, not being quite as subtle as I was, opened the closet door and pulled out a pair of red pumps. "Lovely shoes. Eight and a half. Just my size."

Marilyn blinked a few times. "If I gave you my shoes, I'd have nothing to wear home."

"Oh, I don't want them. Too matronly for me."

Ruthie smiled and sat on a long, padded bench placed there for overnight guests.

"Don't mind her," I explained, frowning. "She's on medication."

"Ah." Marilyn nodded. Since so many stars were on one form of anxiety med or another, no one gave a second thought to that type of explanation.

"I hate to ask this, but…" I put a hand on her arm, "do you have any idea who would want you dead?"

"I can name two off the top of my head. Louie and that wife of his."

"Not Leo?"

She shook her head. "No, that man loves me to a fault and I did him wrong. After this near-death experience, I need to make amends and start over." Tears spilled down her cheeks. "I've lost the baby, so Leo and I can have a fresh start if he'll have me."

"I'm sorry."

"Sin has a price." She closed her eyes. "I'm tired, ladies. Please visit again."

I motioned for Ruthie to follow me.

She shook her head and quietly opened the closet again. "A note," she mouthed.

I stepped to her side and read, "Keep your thoughts to yourself or pay the price. That sounds like a threat to me." I snapped a photo of it with my cell phone. "It also makes it sound like Marilyn might not be a suspect."

"Don't take her off the list yet." Ruthie pointed to a can of spray paint at the bottom of a canvas bag.

Now, I knew there could be a number of reasons why someone might have spray paint in their rather large purse, but the one at the front of my mind was to spray a skull and crossbones on someone's porch. Mine.

"What are you doing?" Marilyn's voice rang out.

"Why do you have a can of spray paint in your purse?" I glared.

"Well, it isn't mine. Do I look like the type of person to go around painting graffiti? The same person who left me that note you read most likely left the paint. Why? I have no idea. Now go."

We went. Back at home, Brock sat on the front porch looking every bit the anxious father waiting for his teenage daughter to arrive home from a date. He got unsteadily to his feet as we got out of the car.

"I expected you back over an hour ago. Do you know how worried I've been?"

I grinned. "You're so cute when you're worried. Come inside, and we'll get you all caught up."

"Hmmph." He held the door open for Ruthie and me to enter.

"Wine, coffee, soda?" Ruthie asked on her way to the kitchen.

"A beer," Brock said.

"Wine for me." I could stand to relax a little. The clues we'd uncovered that day had me wound tight.

I sat on the sofa next to Brock, not resisting when he put his arm around my shoulder and pulled me close. "I really was worried," he said.

"I meant it when I said you were cute."

He chuckled. "Tell me what you found out."

I started with Amber having her second audition and ended with finding the spray paint in Marilyn's purse. "I think she's telling the truth, but she is an actress."

"True," he said. "But, I can't see her sneaking here and painting your porch. That seems more the act of someone who doesn't mind getting their hands dirty."

"Maybe she hired some street kid."

"That is a strong possibility. It did have a graffiti artist vibe."

Which put one more path in my way. There was a group of young men who hung out not far from the Hollywood Walk of Fame. I'd ask them if they knew anything and make sure I had a pocket full of twenties. They wouldn't tell me anything for free.

"I think Marilyn is innocent." Ruthie set a silver tray with wine glasses and a bottle of merlot, along with a beer for Brock, on the coffee table. "I don't think Marilyn would spray the porch. As for hiring someone," she shrugged, "I doubt she'd know the first thing about finding someone to hire. She's one of the biggest snobs I've ever met and would think approaching such a person beneath her. I hate to speak ill of her in her condition, but I'm merely being honest."

I poured a glass of the dark wine and sat back against the sofa cushions. My gaze fell on the photo albums again. "We need to go back through these. Something is bothering me and it has to do with these albums or the photos I took from the awards party."

"No time like the present." Brock took the party pics and handed each of us an album. "When we finish with one, we'll switch so that all three of us look at them all."

I flipped idly through the photo album, stopping on a page of Lauren and a young man frolicking on Huntington Beach. The time stamp was ten years old. I peered closer. "Leo. Give me those pictures." I snatched the award pics from Brock's hand and dropped one-by-one onto his lap. "Here. Look." I tapped the photo then the album. "Leo seems to have been very close to Lauren at one time. Here they seem very much like a couple in love. In this picture, he's talking to Amber and neither one of them look happy. See? In the hallway behind Marilyn and Gary Porter." What a photo bomb!

Brock took the picture back and brought it close

to his eyes. "Neither one of them should have been there in the first place. Makeup artists were supposed to stay back, away from the party. Same with caterers, unless to fill the buffet table or serve drinks. They're too close to the party and Lauren's room to be within the guidelines."

"Who cares about the rules, Brock? We're looking for a woman with a certain size shoe. Tomorrow, I'm going to be looking very closely at Amber's footwear. We also need to talk more with Leo. It's quite possible our killer is a man and it was a woman who did the painting. We could be looking at a murderous couple."

"Now you're really reaching."

"Am not." I quickly flipped back through the album, then slammed it closed. My gut told me there was more information in those pages than I was spotting right off. The killer was in the pictures on the coffee table. We just needed to find the right one.

CHAPTER TWENTY

I had three things on my to-do list that day; see whether any word on the street could be linked to someone hiring a hitman to kill Lauren, talk to Leo, and snoop through Amber's footwear. Item number one stretched before me. A sidewalk with stars portraying actor's names stretched as far as I could see.

Feeling very much like a criminal, I approached someone in a Spiderman costume and waited for the line of eager photo takers to subside. I had my camera around my neck, just in case. You never knew when a star might arrive, and I could make some money selling to a tabloid.

"No photos without paying me a donation of five dollars," Spidey said.

"Then it isn't a donation." I forked over the money. "I'm not here to take your photo. I'm here to ask a question."

"That will cost you another five." He held out

his hand.

"Fine. Can we please step over here away from the tourists?" I motioned around the corner.

"You aren't going to mug me, are you?"

"No." I rolled my eyes. "Besides, who would mug Spiderman?"

"You know I'm not real, right?"

If I rolled my eyes any further, I'd be able to see behind me. Once we were away from the crowd, I turned and crossed my arms. "I'm looking for someone willing to…uh, do a job for money."

He stiffened. "Like a hitman?"

"Exactly!" I grinned. "A street punk, maybe?"

He grabbed me by the arm and pushed me against the wall. "Are you a cop?"

I shook him off. "If I were, I'd arrest you for assaulting a police officer. No, I'm not. My reasons for asking this question are mine alone."

"There's a group of thugs that will do almost anything for money. They aren't professionals, though."

"They still might know something. Thanks." I turned to go when a whimper drew my attention to a dumpster.

"Are we done?"

I waved a dismissive hand toward Spidey and followed the sound. Behind the dumpster sat a cardboard box. Inside that box stood a female German Shepherd puppy. "Oh, sweetie." I picked her up and cradled her in my arms. "Who would dump such a beauty?" I glanced around to see whether the puppy belonged to a homeless person.

Not seeing any signs of anyone living in the near vicinity, I slipped the puppy into my shoulder bag, securing her so she could look out. "I'm going to call you Shutterbug." Ruthie would have a fit, but I'd always wanted a dog and was perfectly capable of caring for one. Besides, if I was going to make a habit of frequenting dangerous places, a guard dog would be a good thing. With my new bestfriend licking my arm, my purse weighing down my left shoulder with it's extra burden, and my camera hanging around my neck, I continued my search for a hired killer.

I knew it was a long shot. I also knew I could be putting a target on my back. But, I was running out of options. I was so close to solving Lauren's murder that I could smell it. No, wait. Yuck. "Shutterbug! You can't go pee-pee in my purse."

"Heard you wanted to hire somebody."

I turned and came face-to-face with an ebony-skinned young man standing six-feet-tall and built like a linebacker. "No, just have some questions." I swallowed past a desert dry throat. "I'm not a cop," I quickly added. "I guess you've spoken to Spiderman."

He gave a sharp nod. "We don't kill people for money. Steal, beat up, yeah, those things, but killing…we draw the line there."

I lowered my voice. "I'm hoping you might know something about the murder of Lauren Mayfield."

"The actress?" He frowned. "Word on the street is that she was killed by one of her own."

"That's it?" My heart sank.

"That's all we know. Look in your own backyard, lady." He turned and marched away.

"Great, girl. It's Leo's next." I hurried to where I'd left my car, set the purse and pup on the front seat, and then drove to the restaurant. I knew the hostess wouldn't allow a dog inside, and I couldn't leave her in the car with the temperature rising, so I hefted the bag and dog onto my shoulder again and snuck through the back door of Leo's.

His office door was open, showing him sitting behind his desk, staring straight ahead. From the glazed look in his eyes, I guessed he really didn't look at anything.

I knocked. "May I come in?"

He blinked a few times, then seemed to come to his senses. "Sure. Have a seat. Oh, a puppy." A smile spread across his face. "Let me hold her."

"She's…wet."

"I don't care. She's good for a breaking heart."

I handed Shutterbug to him and smiled as he baby-talked and gave the puppy kisses. When he settled down, setting my dog in his lap, his hand idly stroking her fur, he glanced at me, "What's up?"

"I've come into possession of Lauren's photo albums," I said, sitting in a leather chair across from him. "Old photos. When the two of you were much younger. You seemed pretty close."

A shadow passed over his eyes. "We were. I wanted to marry her, but stardom was her first priority and I was shoved aside." He gave a wry smile. "I don't seem to have much luck dating actresses, do I?"

I shook my head. "I also have a photo of you at the awards party. It looked as if you were having an argument with Lauren's makeup artist."

He growled deep in his throat. "That girl is like a Pitbull. All I wanted to do was congratulate an old friend on her award and I was denied entrance."

"Did Amber say why she wouldn't let you in?"

"No. But she was acting real sketchy. What if Lauren was already dead?"

I hadn't considered that possibility. I ran through my mind how much time had passed since I'd interviewed her and Brock and when Doug had cried the alarm. Plenty of time for a murder and folks to go on as if nothing had happened.

He leaned closer. "I know you're looking into her death. Have you been to her home? I have a key." He pulled a keyring from a desk drawer and removed a gold key. "I no longer need this."

I held out my hand and he dropped the key into my palm. This was an unexpected gift. Talking to Amber could wait. I'd see her tomorrow for filming anyway. "Thank you, Leo. How's Marilyn?"

"Improving. I'm going to marry her despite her mistakes."

I stood and reached for Shutterbug. "I hope you'll both be very happy." I meant it, too. Leo seemed like a nice guy—if he wasn't the killer. I still had my doubts. Sometimes, as the old cliché went, still waters ran deep, and he had cared greatly for Lauren once upon a time.

I'd just closed the door to my car and settled Shutterbug back in the passenger seat when my cell phone rang. "Hey, Ruthie."

"Where are you? Brock is fit to be tied. When he left his room and you were gone—"

"How would you like to go snooping at Lauren's house?"

"Pick me up." Click.

I laughed. Sometimes my grandmother was more like a toddler than an adult with how easy she was to distract. I moved Shutterbug to the backseat where she promptly curled up and went to sleep.

An hour later, Ruthie having snuck out the backdoor to evade Brock, we pulled up to the iron gate in front of Lauren's mansion. I inserted the key in a keyhole and drove up the winding drive when the gate opened.

A salmon-colored stucco mansion rose above the palm trees. Other desert plants, picked for their beauty and ease of care were placed attractively around the lawn. The remnants of crime scene tape fluttered from a cactus.

"This is nice," Ruthie said.

Shutterbug yelped from the back seat.

Ruthie screamed. "There's a dog in the car."

"She's mine. I've named her Shutterbug."

"Is that why your car smells like someone went to the bathroom in it?"

"She wet in my purse." I opened my car and exited, retrieving Shutterbug from the back and set her on the grass to do her business. "No arguments, Ruthie. I'm keeping her. I found her in a cardboard box next to a dumpster."

Tears welled in my grandmother's eyes. "She was thrown away?"

"It looks that way."

"The poor baby." She tilted her head. "I suppose getting them this small won't be too bad."

"She'll get quite big." I grinned. "She'll be an excellent watchdog."

"Hmmph." Ruthie breathed deeply through her nose, squared her shoulders, and approached the front door of the house. "Let's see what we can see."

The air conditioner had been left on and the great room was pleasantly cool. Floor-to-ceiling windows overlooked a large oval swimming pool. I glanced over to where Shutterbug padded down a hallway. I doubted she could get into much trouble since no one lived there. "I wonder if they're going to sell this place?"

"I wonder if I can afford it." Ruthie stepped up to the French doors, frowning at a smear of fingerprint ink. "I've always wanted to live in Beverly Hills in a place like this."

I shrugged. "It's kind of big for just the two of us, but you won't know if you don't ask."

"I've quite the bank account. Maybe I will." She smiled over her shoulder and headed for the kitchen.

"I'll take this side of the house," I said, turning right.

I came to a bathroom as large as my bedroom. A claw-footed tub, big enough for two people sat in the center of the room. Through an open door, I could see the master suite and a closet any fashionista would die for. I strolled through the bathroom, my fingers grazing the porcelain tub and stepped into the closet.

The walls had been papered with a black and white cheetah print. A plush white carpet covered the floor. A chaise lounge reclined against one wall. The other three were filled with hanging rods, drawers, and shoe shelves filled to the brim.

Shutterbug gave a puppy growl and pulled

something from behind a clothes hamper. I squatted next to her. "What's this?"

She'd dragged out a plastic bag from a supermarket. I couldn't picture Lauren even stepping foot into such a place. I opened the bag and gulped. Inside were a pair of white canvas shoes splattered with red paint. "Good girl, Shutterbug. You're already earning your keep."

Without touching the shoes, I hooked the bag over my arm, scooped up the puppy, and rushed to Ruthie who stared into a cavernous refrigerator.

"This is enormous," she said. "I got distracted."

"Not a problem. Look what I found, or rather, Shutterbug did." I held the bag open.

"Oh, wow. So, who planted them here?"

"What do you mean?" Of course, Lauren didn't kill herself.

"Well, I know for a fact that Lauren had big feet. She wore a size ten."

"How do you know that?"

"Because I wanted to borrow a pair of her shoes. Besides, Kelly…she'd never go grocery shopping. She always ordered it delivered. If she did have to shop for herself, it was always at a more upscale place." She nodded. "Yep, someone planted those there."

"Why?"

She shrugged. "So they wouldn't have to hide them at their place."

I sighed. "The tape had been taken down, meaning the police had done whatever investigating they meant to do. Which means that the shoes were planted here after their search. There's no way they'd have missed them."

"Who gave you the key?"

"Leo." My eyes widened. "Someone else has a key to this place. When you unlock the gate, then the front door, you turn off the alarm."

Ruthie counted names off on her fingers. "Leo, Doug, Amber. Those three would definitely have a key, I think. One of them, is our killer. I really hope it isn't Doug. I like him."

CHAPTER TWENTY-ONE

We returned home to the sight of a stony-faced Brock wearing a boot on his foot instead of using crutches. He slowly got to his feet from the wicker chair on the porch and crossed his arms. "Where have you been?" His gaze flicked to Shutterbug in my arms.

"Uh, asking questions." I flashed the biggest grin I could. "And snooping."

Ruthie shook the paper sack. "Shoes!"

"Where are your crutches?" I asked, trying to move past him.

He blocked my path to the front door. "When I discovered you gone, I called Uber, went to the doctor, and demanded he remove the cast and give me a walking boot. Obviously, I need to be mobile in order to keep an eye on you since you refuse to stay home."

"I have to do this, Brock." I squeezed past, then held Shutterbug up to his face. She licked his nose.

"Meet my new dog. This is Shutterbug. I found her near the Hollywood Walk of Fame."

A smile teased at his lips. "She's adorable. Fine, I'm a sucker for a cute pup. Let's go inside and you tell me what the two of you have been up to without me."

Once inside, Ruthie dramatically dropped the bag with the shoes on the coffee table, scattering the photos we'd left there. As if on cue, the doorbell rang. She glanced outside. "Uh-oh. That detective is here. Shall I hide the evidence?"

"Of course not. We'd have to tell her anyway. Let her in." Knowing how much Shutterbug had softened Brock upon our return, I took her back and cradled her in my arms hoping she'd have the same effect on Lawrence.

Ruthie let Lawrence in. The detective stopped in front of the coffee table, glanced at the scattered photos, then at me. "Cute dog. We'll talk about the pictures in a minute. Would you like to know what caused the accident of Marilyn Clark?"

"Cut brake line?" I raised my eyebrows.

She narrowed her eyes. "How do you know that?"

I shrugged. "She described what happened. It made sense, but now you've confirmed it."

She pressed her lips together in an obvious attempt at controlling her temper. After a few taut seconds where I thought perhaps her head would explode like a cartoon character, she took a deep breath. "Do those photo albums belong to the deceased?"

"Yes. Her trailer is now my trailer and I thought they'd come in handy." I set Shutterbug on the floor. "My hunch was right. We've discovered that Leo Staletti was once in a relationship with Lauren and to this day had a key to her house. We also found out that Leo and Amber Jacobson argued outside Lauren's room when she may, or may not have, already been dead." Feeling quite pleased with myself, I propped my feet on the table and leaned back with a smile.

"I visited Leo who gave me a key to Lauren's home, which Ruthie wants to purchase when it goes on the market." I thought visiting under the pretense of buying the house would go over better than snooping. "While we were there, my dog found what I believe are the shoes the person who spray painted my porch wore." I held up a finger as Lawrence started to speak. "I know they can't be Lauren's, which means someone with a key to her house planted them there. Doug, Leo, or Amber." I couldn't help but feel very brilliant and very much like the investigative reporter I dreamed of being.

"I really think you've missed your calling, Canyon." Lawrence peered in the paper sack. "I'll take these and the photo albums, thank you. I'll also be visiting the three people you named and would appreciate it if you didn't tip them off that I was coming." She glanced at Brock. "You aren't much of a watchdog, are you?"

"Hey, I've got a broken leg." He scowled. "I'll stay on them better with this." He pointed at his boot.

She nodded. "You've done enough, Canyon. I'm very appreciative. Now, focus on your movie and let this remain in my hands." She gathered up the sack and the albums before marching out the door.

"I don't suppose you're going to listen to her?" Brock asked.

"I've been very careful. Now, I've got Shutterbug to warn me if anyone comes around."

"She's a puppy. Most likely she isn't over twelve weeks old." He shook his head. "She might serve that purpose in the future, but not right now. So," he rubbed his hands together, "you don't go anywhere without me from now on. Where do you want go?"

"Does anyone know where Amber lives? I know for a fact she's got another audition today."

"I know how to find out." Ruthie pressed buttons on her cell phone. "Doug, sweetie, could you give me Amber's address? I promised her I'd stop by for something." She smiled and scribbled an address on a slip of paper. "Thanks, love." She hung up. "Voila. I got the info without telling a single lie."

"Did you promise Amber you'd stop by?"

"Sure. Weeks ago. I just never did." She grabbed her purse. "Lock the puppy in the bathroom, Kelly. We don't want her leaving any evidence we were there." She eyed a wet stain on her oriental rug. "Oh, that's wine. I need to call a cleaner."

"I'll still leave her here." I scooped up the puppy and settled her on a plush pillow in the downstairs bathroom. I set out a small bowl of water. "I'll be back soon, sweetie."

Amber lived in an older neighborhood that might once have been nice. Now, homes had been divided into duplexes with small yards covered with concrete parking. I stared at the faded red door of number eleven. "How do you propose we get in?"

"Move aside, dear." Ruthie pulled a felt pouch from her purse. "Don't ask. I borrowed from a friend." She knelt and proceeded to pick the lock as if she'd been committing crime her entire life.

"You have to teach me how to do that." I grinned. "If I make it a habit to help solve mysteries, that skill will come in handy."

"God, spare me from crazy women." Brock leaned against the wall. "I suggest you hurry before someone gets suspicious."

"There." Ruthie stood and turned the door handle.

The door swung open easily into a clean apartment. The furniture was outdated, but in good condition. Throw rugs covered a tiled floor. A tiny kitchen was to our left, a bedroom to our right. A closed door, which I assumed was the bathroom, was straight ahead.

I turned right, Ruthie went straight, leaving the kitchen for Brock. "We're looking for anything related to Lauren or Marilyn," I said.

A navy-blue and white striped comforter covered a queen-sized bed. A shaker-style dresser and nightstand were the only other pieces of furniture. Amber was more of a minimalist than most people I knew.

I opened a small walk-in closet. Here was where she spent her money. The rods were so packed with clothes, some she could only have gotten from Lauren, that the rods sagged and clothes were jammed together. Evening gowns, tee-shirts, jeans…all together with no thought to organization. I felt of a silk gown the color of daffodils. Amber was larger than Lauren. Was she hoping to one day lose weight?

A small battered suitcase adorned with travel stamps sat on the crowded shelf over the clothes. I pulled it down and released the latch. Posters of movies Lauren starred in, head shots of Amber, and a journal lay inside. I flipped through the journal, stopping whenever I saw a mention of Lauren's name. Amber may have been her makeup artist, and acted bereaved upon hearing of her death, but according to the journal, Lauren hadn't been optimistic in regard to Amber's acting skills.

The sound of the front door opening and Amber's shrill voice asking what were we doing in her apartment, had me scurrying to put the items back in the suitcase and on the shelf. I pasted a smile onto my face and stepped into the living room. "How did your audition go?"

"How did you get in here?"

"The door was unlocked," Ruthie said. "We came to support you. Well?"

Amber glanced from me, to Ruthie, to Brock. "I think I got the part. It's a small one, but it's a start. I play the friend to the female role so will have a walk on or two each episode. You really came to see how I did?"

"You bet." Ruthie clapped her on the shoulder. "I'm glad it went well. See you on the lot tomorrow. Final day of filming."

Amber blinked like an owl. "You're leaving?"

"Lots to do in preparation of the premier."

"Premier of what?" Amber wasn't stupid. She knew the movie we were filming wouldn't premier for at least a year.

"My movie." Brock grinned. "I'm no longer a suspect and edits have been given top priority. Premier is in three months."

"That is fast."

"They've been losing money. Gotta go." He ushered me and Ruthie out the door, flashed a heart-stopping grin in Amber's direction, and then pulled the door closed. "That was close," he said.

"What happens when there is no premier?"

"There will be. They've already edited everything filmed before Lauren's death and finished filming before I broke my leg. It's a rush job, so here's hoping it'll be good." He slid into the passenger seat, while I got behind the wheel. Ruthie pouted, but got in back.

While we drove home, I explained about Amber's feelings toward Lauren. "Then, when you add in Marilyn's accident, it seems plausible that Amber might very well have acted rashly. After all, who premeditates murder with a crab leg?"

"But, if it is Amber," Brock said, "the cutting of Marilyn's brake lines would definitely have been premeditated. We're dealing with someone not quite working with a full deck, if you know what I mean."

"Amber's motive would be anger and hurt feelings. Leo's might be a broken heart. Doug…"I glanced in the rearview mirror at Ruthie.

"He was a bit put out about her cheating," she said in a low voice. "People have killed for less."

"Don't forget that he's the one who found the body," Brock pointed out.

"I wish there was a way to get our three suspects in one place, then bring up the murder."

"Let's have a dinner party in the same place as the award's party." Ruthie leaned on the front seat. "It won't be a problem at all to rent it. Then, we have our suspects in the same place and the place it happened. We can turn it into a tribute, of sorts."

"You are brilliant, Grandma!"

She cleared her throat.

"Sorry. I forget when I'm excited."

"I think it will work," Brock said. "I also think we should have the detectives hanging in the background, just in case."

"Stop being such a scaredy-cat." Ruthie slapped his arm. "No one will be their true self with the police around."

He glared over his shoulder. "I don't want anything to happen to you or Kelly. With this boot on, I couldn't run after a killer, or away from one, if my life depended on it. Which it very well might."

CHAPTER TWENTY-TWO

A week later on Saturday evening, I strolled up a rolled out red carpet, my arm linked with Brock. My entrance this time was so different than that night that seemed so long ago. Pearls adorned my neck instead of a camera strap. Heels that matched my black gown covered my feet instead of gym shoes.

Ruthie, looking radiant in a royal blue gown, had her arm linked with Brock's other one. She looked as glowing as if she were going to accept an award rather than confront a killer. Maybe someday there would be an award with her name on it.

I spotted Susan in the crowd of reporters and paparazzi. She glared my way, but motioned for her cameraman to take our picture anyway. Good girl. No sense in letting personal feelings get in the way of professionalism.

Two men in tuxes opened the front doors wide for us to enter and I was slapped in the face with de ja vu. I'd entered through the back doors last time, but the room looked the same all the way down to the same food on the buffet table and the same servers carrying silver trays. I glanced up at Brock. "You really nailed every detail."

"If we're doing this, we might as well do it right." He smiled at a camera, his arm slipping around my waist.

I grinned for the cameras and breathed deep of his cologne. The warmth of his hand seeped through the silk of my gown, making me very aware of his closeness. I still found it hard to believe that the handsome Brock Hanson chose to spend time with me.

I spotted Amber scowling and leaning against the far wall. She wore black slacks and a sparkly black blouse, clearly feeling out of place. An actress now, she probably still felt like nothing more than a makeup artist watching the famous people play. I slipped free from Brock's arm and made my way to Amber.

"Are you having fun?"

She shook her head. "No one will talk to me. I haven't," she added in finger quotes, " 'made it yet'." I have to pay dues, I guess." She raked her gaze over me. "Of course, it didn't take you long since you're glued to Mr. Handsome."

"Feeling a bit snarky, are you?" I rolled my eyes.

Her face darkened. "Not everything comes as easy as acting did to you. You literally had a part handed to you."

"True, but it's in my blood, I guess. Come on. Let's get something to eat. Did you see the crab legs?"

She flinched. "I couldn't…not after…"

I motioned to where Leo stood next to the buffet table. "What were the two of you arguing about the night Lauren died?"

"What?"

"I was flipping through the pictures I took that night and saw one of the two of you, in that hallway. It looked like you were arguing."

"He wanted to visit Lauren and she specifically told me no visitors. She was upset about not winning Best Actress and had a headache. Satisfied?" She stormed ahead of me.

I rushed to catch up. "So, you planted yourself outside of her room as a guard dog?"

She wrinkled her nose. "In so many words, I guess so."

"Did you stand there from the very moment she told you no visitors? Did you leave at all?"

"Yes and no. What are you getting at, Kelly?"

I exhaled heavily. "If you were there all night, then no one could have gotten into—"

"Kelly." Susan waved for me to come over.

"Excuse me, Amber. I'll be back." I joined

Susan on the other side of the room. "I was in the middle of questioning a suspect."

She grabbed my arm and pulled me toward the bathroom. "I overheard something. Come with me."

"Slow down. I can't run in heels." I hiked my gown above my ankles and tottered after her as fast as I could without breaking an ankle.

As soon as we were inside the bathroom, she turned the lock on the door. "Okay. I overheard Leo and Doug talking about Lauren. Both of them loved her very much, and they both seem to have moved on. A bit sudden, but it is Hollywood."

"This doesn't mean anything."

She tilted her head. "The part I found strange about the conversation was that they seemed to be trying to outdo each other on how much they loved her. What if they were in competition and she chose unwisely?"

"I have my number one suspect and it isn't one of them." She really wasn't good at investigating, which, God forgive me, sent a thrill of pleasure up my spine. I couldn't believe I'd been worried about her winning the silly competition with the Tribune.

"Who is it?"

"I'm not going to tell you."

"You're lying. You don't have a clue."

"I do."

She shook her head. "You have a strong inclination. That isn't the same." She reached for the door handle.

"Look, Susan. I have people around me constantly. You can't go investigating this murder alone. It's too dangerous."

Her eyes sparked. "Too dangerous for me, but not for you? Right." She unlocked the door. "I'll find that killer before you do."

I leaned my back against the cool marble of the sink. I was helping Lawrence, even after she'd told me she no longer needed my help. Susan was rushing into a possible dangerous situation blind, and I had no idea how to keep her from doing it.

The best I could do was keep an eye on her during the party. I left the bathroom and searched the banquet hall for not only Susan, but for Amber. Susan stood across from me questioning Leo. Amber was nowhere in sight. So much for continuing our conversation.

"Where have you been?" Brock stepped up behind me. "Doug is fit to be tied. He stepped into Lauren's room and collapsed. Ruthie is trying to console him, but he says he can't get the picture of Lauren lying on the sofa out of his mind."

"Because he stabbed her perhaps?" I didn't think so, but until I had a confession, he was still in my top three suspects.

By now, a crowd had gathered around Lauren's old room. Doug sat on the sofa, face in his hands, Ruthie beside him. She looked up at me helplessly.

"He's really hung up on her."

I could see the pain in her eyes. My poor grandmother. Since the death of Grandpa she'd been unlucky in the love department.

Flashbulbs went off behind me. Brock turned and ordered everyone back and for them to give the man some privacy.

"This is a good story," Susan said, refusing to move. "It will sell papers."

Amber stepped in front of the camera. "Not this time." She put her hand over the lens. "Come back later."

"Cut it out." Leo barged into the room. "Look." He pointed at Doug. "Not a single tear. He's still trying to prove he loved her more."

"Are you two for real?" I glared at them both. "A woman was brutally murdered by someone in this room and you're having some kind of silly rooster competition, strutting your ruffled feathers in front of the camera and witnesses." I put my fists on my hips. "You shame her by your behavior." With those words, I turned and exited the room, leaving stunned silence behind me.

Well-liked or not, Lauren didn't deserve a circus. It was a bad idea having the party. It wasn't like the killer would make an announcement. I snatched a strawberry from the buffet table and swirled it in cream before popping it into my mouth.

"You're right." Brock approached me. "They're

acting like fools. No man in love would desecrate the memory of the woman he cherished in that way. At least I wouldn't."

"There aren't many men like you left." I gazed into his eyes.

He gave a crooked smile. "There are more of us then you know, but I'm glad I'm the one you ran across."

"That was quite the little speech," Susan said coming up behind us. "You've turned into quite the dramatic one."

"There's nothing dramatic about the truth." I stepped back from Brock.

"The truth is more dramatic than anything. So, who killed Lauren?"

I caught a quick glimpse of Lawrence and Sawyer wearing caterer uniforms disappear behind the swinging doors of the kitchen. I groaned. If the killer caught sight of them, they'd run. "Who called them?" I motioned with my head.

"I did." Brock sighed. "They weren't invited, only given a heads up."

"Which got them in the door. This could ruin everything."

"This could save you from a dangerous situation."

Susan's head swiveled back and forth between us so fast it was a wonder it didn't come unhinged and roll across the floor. "Brock is solving the crime, too? Is there anyone not trying to find the killer?"

"Yeah," I glared. "The killer." I marched for the kitchen and barged through the doors. "You're ruining my plan."

"You. Are. Not. A. Cop." Lawrence pointed at my head. "Remember that."

"You asked for my help."

"I told you to step down."

"Ugh." I whirled and stomped away, heading for the storage room in back where I could hopefully find a few moments to sort through my thoughts.

I sat on a cardboard box and toed off my heels. I planted my feet flat on the cool marble surface and rested my elbows on my knees and my chin in my hands. I was failing miserably. I'd had the same three suspects forever. The same three the detectives had. How silly of me to think that having daily access to the studio lot gave me more skills than the professionals.

The lights blinked out leaving me in utter blackness. I sat still for a moment, then got slowly to my feet. With my hands stretched out in front of me, I headed for the door.

Someone breathed to my right, their breath tickling the hair on my neck.

I froze, biting my tongue to keep from saying, "Who's there?" like every Too Stupid To Live girl in the horror flicks. I held my breath and took another step toward where I thought the door was.

"Not one little peep, Kelly." Something sharp poked me in the side.

CHAPTER TWENTY-THREE

"So, I was right." Even in the face of imminent danger, I smiled. "You are the killer. I was just about to confront you."

"Liar," Amber said, jabbing me with the object again. "You suspected, that's all. Now move or I will shoot you here in the closet."

"Where are we going?"

"Somewhere fitting." She prodded me out the door.

I glanced both ways, my eyes starting to adjust to the darkness. Not a single person was in the kitchen. From the noise on the other side of the swinging doors it was obvious where everyone was. "What did you do?"

"I created a distraction. Very clever of me to put a mannequin in Lauren's room in the very pose her body was found in, don't you think?"

"You're sick."

"No, just very determined to accomplish my dreams." We stepped outside to where a van idled. Amber ordered me in the back where a very frightened looking Susan sat tied up.

A hard knock to the back of my head and darkness overcame me.

I woke to my hands zip-tied together and a duct tape over my mouth. The smart woman had also stuck my shoes a few feet away out of my reach. Poop. I had planned on sinking one of the heels into the top of her foot.

The van door slid open. "Get out," Amber ordered. "We're back where it all began."

The studio. I recognized the set as being from Lauren's first movie. One where she played a reporter lost in a South American jungle. A low budget movie not filmed on location but in a jungle of silk and plastic foliage. I'd seen the same set on a few children's movies, but hadn't really expected such an elaborate set-up. The jungle filled an entire warehouse.

"Move to those rocks over there next to the creek." Amber waved a hand gun at us.

With a quick glance at Susan, I led the way. Amber disappeared for a minute, but returned seconds after the water feature of a small waterfall and creek started up. Then, she sat across from us. "I haven't been entirely truthful with you."

I made a noise behind my tape.

"Sorry." She yanked it off, taking skin with it.

"That hurt," I spit between gritted teeth.

She shrugged. "Not as much as this bullet will when I shoot you."

Susan whimpered, drawing Amber's attention to her. "You're just collateral damage. If you hadn't been asking questions in the ladies' room you wouldn't be here." Amber grinned. "You should really check the stalls before having a secret conversation."

Like an idiot I'd assumed Susan had checked. I wouldn't make that mistake again. "What's your lie?" Keep her talking, right? Give help time to arrive. It wouldn't take Detective Lawrence long to figure out I'd disappeared. The problem would be in finding where I'd been taken.

My clutch. I'd had it with me. God, please let it be in the van. If so, they could trace it, right? I really needed to get a better education on technical issues.

"My current acting job isn't my first. I'm sure by now you recognize this place." Amber glanced around us. "Remember the ape who peered through the bushes at the heroine? That was me. Poor, spoiled, Lauren hadn't wanted to lose her wonderful makeup artist so she sabotaged my career. Ruined my self-esteem. It wasn't until I found her sad and alone in her dressing room that it all came to a head." Amber sighed. "Five years it took me to get my revenge."

"Why didn't you just quit?"

She narrowed her eyes. "I'm not a quitter, Kelly. I'm a good makeup artist and the movie world is a small one. I just had to wait until Lauren was as vulnerable as I'd been."

I didn't buy it. "There has to be more to your reasoning, Amber."

"Fine, but it's so high school cliché that it's embarrassing. She took the man I loved away from me."

"Doug?"

"Eew."

"Leo? Louie?"

"Don't be ridiculous. The leading man on this film."

My blood ran cold. "Brock?" I was pretty sure he had no idea of Amber's feelings for him.

"Ding, ding, ding, we have a winner. Now, it seems my love is infatuated with you. But I'll be a star soon and with you out of the picture, I'll be there to comfort him." Her smile reminded me of a shark.

"But, Brock and I aren't dating, Amber. You may have seen us in the tabloids but that was just publicity. Surely you understand that."

"There is still the fact that you know I killed Lauren and tried to kill Marilyn."

"All because you want to be a star."

"Because they tried to prevent my dream from happening." Her eyes hardened. "I really liked you, Kelly. Ruthie, too. She is going to be very sad, and I'm sorry about that."

"There's no reason to do this, Amber." I kept my gaze locked on hers. "Untie us and let us go. We can chalk all this off to a moment of temporary insanity. You'll be prescribed—"

"I'm not crazy!"

"I didn't say that. Maybe," I raised my bound hands, "depressed?"

"I ought to shoot you now." She raised the gun.

I swallowed past the cactus in my throat.

Susan whimpered, tears running down her cheeks.

"But, I thought we could play a game." Amber's smile remained in place. "I'm the bad guy out to hunt down the heroine. Remember that part in the movie? Where the ape got killed instead of the heroine? Well, the two of you are the apes. Run."

It wasn't until she shouted the word that I realized she was serious. Susan and I bolted to our feet and staggered into the plastic forest. How long did we have before a bullet buried itself between our shoulder blades?

Susan stopped behind a concrete post made to look like a tree and reached up to peel off her tape. "What do we do?"

"I don't know. I'm not familiar with this set

other than seeing it in in a movie." I searched the area around us. "We need a place to hide." Not that any place would keep Amber from finding us, but if we kept wandering, we were bound to come across her. Staying put might buy us some time.

"Helloooo?" Amber's voice rang through the building. "Are we having fun?"

"She's nuts," Susan hissed. "You can have Lauren's story. I'm writing about this crack head."

"If we don't make it out alive, we won't have to worry about a story." I parted some silk fern branches and shoved Susan inside. "Stay down." I covered myself with a bush across from her, thankful my dress was dark. At least it would appear like shadows at first glance, I hoped.

I wrapped my bound hands around my knees and rested my chin on them. I wanted to close my eyes and make it all go away like I did as a child. If I couldn't see someone, they couldn't see me.

Maybe I wasn't cut out to be an investigative journalist. If I did pursue that occupation, there might be other times my life was in danger, and being honest, I wasn't having fun.

I held my breath as Amber strolled by, humming a catchy tune. Once she'd passed, I crawled closer to where the water feature was. If I was lucky, it would take her some time before she circled all the way around.

Susan's wide eyes peered through the plants and

she followed me.

When I reached the waterfall, I turned in the direction I thought the door we entered through was. If we could find our way out, I could retrieve my phone and call for help. I put a finger to my lips and keeping low, veered right.

Before stepping clear of the last of the movie set, I shot out my arm and stopped Susan. Amber anticipated our move and waited next to the double steel doors. This woman was really beginning to annoy me.

I melted back into the set and contemplated my next move. If only I could free my hands. I reached up as I'd seen in the movies and brought them down swift and hard to break the ties. All I succeeded in doing was cutting my wrists. I bit back a scream and tried again.

The ties broke away. Tears sprang to my eyes. Now my hands were free to throttle Amber. My fingers curved into position.

Amber studied her nails on the hand holding the gun. She frowned. "I did think they'd try to escape," she muttered. "I guess Kelly isn't as bright as I thought she was." She straightened. "I'm getting bored, ladies. Here I come. This time, I will find you." She turned to her left.

I bolted for the door.

A shot rang out, chipping paint from the wall beside my head.

I dove to the side.

Another shot rang out.

Susan screamed.

I looked up in time to see her crumble to the floor.

Amber, still grinning, approached her.

It was now or never. I sprang to my feet and charged.

CHAPTER TWENTY-FOUR

I rammed into Amber, taking her to the floor with me. The gun skittered from her hand and under a fake palm tree. We grappled for each other's hands.

Her nail scraped my cheek.

"Not the face!" I still had filming to do. I doubled up my fist and connected with the side of her head.

She cursed and reached for my throat.

A loud banging on the steel doors made us freeze, but only for a second before we continued rolling around on fake dirt like a couple of professional wrestlers. I half-way registered the fact that Susan managed to stumble to the doors and slide the bolt before slipping back to the floor.

A pair of arms wrapped around my waist and pulled me off Amber. I turned and swung, barely stopping in time to prevent a punch from connecting with Brock's jaw. While he pulled me into an embrace, Sawyer cuffed Amber and Lawrence phoned for an ambulance.

"How did you find us?" I asked, my voice muffled against the reassuring, comforting feel of Brock's chest.

"They traced your phone." He pushed my hair away from my face. "I liked it up in a stylish twist, but with it mussed and hanging around your face, your dress torn…" his lips curled into a smile, "you're the sexiest thing I've ever seen." His finger traced the scratch on my cheek.

"This was all because she's loved you since you made a movie here."

"What?" He frowned.

"She was the ape you shot." I rested my forehead back on his chest. "Then, when she thought Lauren stole you and also sabotaged her career, she plotted revenge."

"Thanks for clearing that up." Lawrence stood next to us. "Do you need medical attention?"

I shook my head. "How's Susan?"

"Lucky for her, Amber Jacobson is a bad shot. The bullet grazed her shoulder." Lawrence glanced around us. "Only in Hollywood would an attempted murder occur on a movie set." She rubbed her hands together. "Let's wrap this up. I need a drink."

Brock put his arm around my shoulder and led me to a waiting limo. "I would've driven myself, but the boot kind of prevents me from driving."

I laughed. "Only in Hollywood is a girl who was almost murdered picked up in a limo." I loved this town.

The driver opened the rear door for us. I climbed in first. "My purse and shoes."

Brock clomped his way to the van and retrieved my items. "Can't forget the accessories."

"Not a chance. These things cost a lot of money." I slid over so he could join me on the seat. With the adrenaline draining from my body, exhaustion quickly took its place. "Where's my grandmother?"

"Anxiously waiting at home. Lawrence refused to let her come since she was hysterical." He pulled me close to his side. "I promised to bring you home."

"I'm very glad you get to keep that promise." I snuggled into the curve of his shoulder and closed my eyes.

Brock shook me awake when the limo pulled in front of the house. I opened my eyes to the sight of Ruthie rushing down the sidewalk toward us.

"My girl." She clutched me to her the moment I climbed from the limo. "I was so scared." She held me at arm's length. "You're a mess." She pulled me close again. "Come inside. I'll fix you a hot bath and pour you a glass of wine."

"Just the bath."

"Fine. The wine is for me." She laughed and

took my hand. "No more chasing killers."

"No promises." I grinned. Now that the threat of danger was over, I realized I'd loved the rush of helping justice be served. Yes, my father's blood ran strong in my veins.

True to her word, Ruthie fixed me a bath, filled it with fragrant bubbles, then sat on a stool after I slid under the water. "I want you to keep acting, Kelly, or being paparazzi. I can't lose you to a madman like I lost my only son." Her eyes shimmered. "I thought finding Lauren's killer would be fun, and it was at times, but when you were taken…well, it brought home all those old fears."

I filled my hand with bubbles and contemplated her words. I fully understood, having lived through the same loss. But rather than want to run from it, I wanted to help make the world a better place and see justice served. My father's killer died in prison. A fitting end to a cold-blooded drug dealer. I blew the bubbles off my palms.

"The feeling that knowing Lauren's death was solved, that her family has closure, is something I want to experience again. Would it make you feel better if I promised to take self-defense classes and learn to shoot?" I cut her a sideways glance.

"No." Her brow furrowed. "Your father knew those things and they didn't help him." She shook her head and stood. "You're an adult. I can't stop you. Chances are, I'll feel differently when, and if, another mystery prevents itself." She wagged a finger at me. "I can tell you that I'll be praying long and hard that another one doesn't. You also need to train that puppy. She has no idea what 'go outside' means."

I chuckled as she left me alone. I hoped no one else died, too. I wouldn't want a death just so I could have my adrenaline rush. I rested my head back against the porcelain edge of the tub. I still planned on pursuing my reporter dream, and continuing to make money snapping photos of celebrities, but maybe actually acting for a living would be the safest. Then, I could do as Dad did. Save the money I made from acting and quit to pursue what I really wanted to do without worrying about how I'd pay the bills.

I smiled, knowing I had a plan for the future. While I soaked, I thought of the article I'd start writing in the morning.

CHAPTER TWENTY-FIVE

Six months later

Again, I strolled the red carpet on Brock's arm as cameras flashed around us. Despite my previous reluctance to live the Hollywood lifestyle, I found I actually enjoyed the attention once I got used to it.

While we were attending the premier of Brock's latest film, finishing up the one I'd been thrust into turned out to be one of the most satisfying and rewarding things I'd ever done. The Tribune wanted to hire me back after I'd written the article, but I declined and decided to turn the article into a book instead. I'd written The End yesterday.

Ruthie joked that I was still a child who didn't know what I wanted to be when I grew up. Maybe she was right. Actor, author, photographer, journalist…they were all a part of me. Maybe, someday, I'd pick one. Right now, I loved my life and wouldn't change a thing.

We sat in plush red velvet seats and watched Brock play a jaded detective who is framed for the murder of a young woman. I'd known he was good, but seeing him in a serious, action-type role showed just how good he was. I glanced at his handsome profile.

Kind, modest, and good at what he chose for his career. While the paparazzi often paired us together as a romantic couple, we'd never said exactly what our relationship was. For now, I'd be content with friendship.

After the show, we moved to the same banquet hall that had sent me on the dangerous path of solving Lauren's murder. To Ruthie's comfort, I'd not had another mystery thrust at me.

I stood in the doorway of what was once Lauren's dressing room, or rather a room where she could escape the crowds. The sofa she'd died on had been replaced with one in navy-blue. Nothing was the same. Life went on. I hadn't liked the woman, not really, but to see how easily a person could be erased was disheartening.

"She's really gone for good." Doug stepped into the room. "I can't thank you enough for giving everyone closure."

"The police would have solved the case soon. I just happened to say the wrong thing to the wrong person." I still checked the bathroom stalls whenever I entered a ladies' room. I ran my hand over the sofa. "Her last movie did well at the box office."

"Unfortunately, murder sells almost as well as sex."

"Hmm." I drew breath sharply through my nose. "Now what?"

"For me?" He grinned. "I'm free to pursue Ruthie. I've said my goodbyes to Lauren, and your grandmother will never give me reason to think her unfaithful."

"She is a good woman." I speared him with a glance. "Don't do her wrong."

"Never."

Brock leaned against the doorframe and gave me the slow, lazy smile that almost sent my heart into overdrive. "Ready to go home? Ruthie said Shutterbug is scratching at the door."

I rolled my eyes. Now that the German Shepherd was almost full grown, Ruthie acted afraid of her to the point she wouldn't even open the back door of the mansion she'd bought so the dog could go outside. "I really need to have a doggie door put in."

"Has Ruthie agreed to let you?"

"Not yet." I linked my arm with his. At first, moving into Lauren's former home had seemed eerie, but once we removed all her things and remodeled, it was a beautiful home and Ruthie was happy. "But she did say I could put French doors in my bedroom. I'll install the doggie door then."

"Trouble maker."

"You have no idea."

"I think I do. The last few months have shown me exactly what type of girl I hang with." He leaned over and kissed me. "On to new adventures?"

"Definitely."

Check out book 2, Killer Snapshot, by scanning this code.

236

www.cynthiahickey.com

Cynthia Hickey is a multi-published and best-selling author of cozy mysteries and romantic suspense. She has taught writing at many conferences and small writing retreats. She and her husband run the publishing press, Winged Publications. They live in Arizona and Arkansas, becoming snowbirds with three dogs. They have ten grandchildren who keep them busy and tell everyone they know that "Nana is a writer."

Connect with me on FaceBook
Twitter
Amazon
Sign up for my newsletter and receive a free short story
www.cynthiahickey.com

Follow me on Amazon

Enjoy other books by Cynthia Hickey

Time Travel
The Portal

Shady Acres Mysteries
Beware the Orchids, book 1
Path to Nowhere
Poison Foliage
Poinsettia Madness

Deadly Greenhouse Gases
Vine Entrapment

CLEAN BUT GRITTY

Highland Springs

Murder Live
Say Bye to Mommy

Colors of Evil Series

Shades of Crimson
Coral Shadows

The Pretty Must Die Series

Ripped in Red, book 1
Pierced in Pink, book 2
Wounded in White, book 3
Worthy, The Complete Story

Lisa Paxton Mystery Series

Eenie Meenie Miny Mo
Jack Be Nimble
Hickory Dickory Dock

One Hour (A short story thriller)

INSPIRATIONAL
(scroll down to see clean books without inspirational
message)

Whisper Sweet Nothings (a short romance)

Nosy Neighbor Series
Anything For A Mystery, Book 1
A Killer Plot, Book 2
Skin Care Can Be Murder, Book 3
Death By Baking, Book 4
Jogging Is Bad For Your Health, Book 5
Poison Bubbles, Book 6
A Good Party Can Kill You, Book 7 (Final)
Nosy Neighbor collection

Christmas with Stormi Nelson

The Summer Meadows Series
Fudge-Laced Felonies, Book 1
Candy-Coated Secrets, Book 2
Chocolate-Covered Crime, Book 3
Maui Macadamia Madness, Book 4
All four novels in one collection

The River Valley Mystery Series
Deadly Neighbors, Book 1
Advance Notice, Book 2
The Librarian's Last Chapter, Book 3

All three novels in one collection

Historical cozy
Hazel's Quest

Historical Romances
Runaway Sue
Taming the Sheriff
Sweet Apple Blossom

Finding Love the Harvey Girl Way
Cooking With Love
Guiding With Love
Serving With Love
Warring With Love
All 4 in 1

A Wild Horse Pass Novel
They Call Her Mrs. Sheriff, book 1 (A Western Romance)

Finding Love in Disaster
The Rancher's Dilemma
The Teacher's Rescue
The Soldier's Redemption

Woman of courage Series

A Love For Delicious

Ruth's Redemption
Charity's Gold Rush
Mountain Redemption
Woman of Courage series (all four books)

Short Story Westerns
Desert Rose
Desert Lilly
Desert Belle
Desert Daisy
Flowers of the Desert 4 in 1

Romantic Suspense

Overcoming Evil series
Mistaken Assassin
Captured Innocence
Mountain of Fear
Exposure at Sea
A Secret to Die for
Collision Course
Romantic Suspense of 5 books in 1

The Game
Suspicious Minds

Contemporary

Romance in Paradise
Maui Magic

Sunset Kisses
Deep Sea Love
3 in 1

Finding a Way Home

Service of Love

Christmas

Handcarved Christmas
The Payback Bride
Curtain Calls and Christmas Wishes
Christmas Gold
A Christmas Stamp

The Red Hat's Club (Contemporary novellas)

Finally
Suddenly
Surprisingly
The Red Hat's Club 3 – in 1

Short Story

One Hour (A short story thriller)
Whisper Sweet Nothings (a Valentine short romance)